My eyes are tired. I have sat u
scribbling onto this pad as if in a frenzy, wanting to get it all out in
case it slips away like mist.

I make my way to my room, undress, and climb into bed,
propping my pillows up against the headboard, bending my knees to
have something to lean my writing pad on.

My head feels fuzzy at remembering the encounter with my
mother. I did not tell my father that she had called round, wanting to
shield him from it, as I was sure it would taint his now serene life, and
I did not want to spoil that by causing him any pain.

Looking back, what I did next was inevitable. The chain of events
that followed Mother's visit was God's instruction, and there was no
way I was going to ignore Him.

My mind clears now and becomes sharp. I recall just what I *did* do
next. The excitement begins building within me, and I feel fully
awake, knowing that I will jangle for you now, those very chains of
events that followed that stupid woman's visit.

Other works by M. E Ellis available through Wild Child Publishing:

Quits

Praise for Pervalism

"*Pervalism...* is American Psycho, the good parts edition... You like Stephen King, trust me you will love this. This book is what independent publishing is all about: making books that no one else would touch."

Gabriel Llanas, Dred Magazine

"*Pervalism* is deeply disturbing. For much of his life John seems so normal to those who know and love him. This fact makes his acts that much more shocking. That many of the killings evolved from curiosity, exploration, and fascination is just plain traumatizing."

Tami Brady, TCM Reviews

Other titles offered by Wild Child Publishing at http://www.wildchildpublishing.com/, include:

Odd Pursuits by Robert Castle
Quits by M. E Ellis
Soul Haven by Sonja Baines – October 2006 release
Decimate, Vol. I by various authors – October 2006 release
Captives by L-J Baker – November 2006 release
Skinwalker by Matt Hulls – January 2007 release

Pervalism

by

M.E Ellis

Wild Child Publishing.com
Culver City, California

ISBN: 0-9771314-6-7 - ebook
ISBN: 1-934069-21-3 – print

Wild Child Publishing.com
P.O. Box 4897
Culver City, CA 90231-4897

Printed in The United States of America

For Michael Kay

Chapter One

Whenever I picked up snails they would try to hide inside the homes on their backs. I couldn't see their bodies then, so I would rip their houses away. Failing that, I would quite simply stamp on them.

***

I began my life as countless others, born in a hospital to a mother and father who were still married. I was taken home to a modest house, where my parents struggled to pay the mortgage and bills. You could say I had the same chances as any other child born under such circumstances. From the outside, I looked like a boy from any normal family.

My first memory is of toddling, probably around age three, with snails clasped in my chubby hands, bashing their shells against one another. I recall plonking myself down on the grass in our back garden, peeling away the broken bits of snail shell to reveal the squiggly body beneath.

Do snails feel pain? I don't know, but I revelled in that task and remembered digging my thumbnails in their slug-like bodies to try and pierce their tough skin.

My mother admonished me for my snail torture. She shook me and picked me up roughly by the top of my arms, digging her own sharp nails into the soft skin of my underarm. I wondered then if this was what the snails experienced at my hands.

"Go and put those snails in the bush, you little fucker, and then get indoors for your tea!"

I stared defiantly at my mother and measured her up in my own eyes. She had shoulder length hair that was abundant in brown waves, falling back from her face. Hands on her slim waist, her pretty face scowled down on me as if I was the devil incarnate. I wondered why she looked at me that way. Why didn't she look at me the way my father did?

I slung the snails away, not in the bush, but at her painted toenails, and stomped indoors, all the way to the sink—where I washed my hands like the good boy I was supposed to be.

Tea was good. Not only did I get bread and butter, but if I was lucky, jam as well. Maybe a biscuit would follow, and a glass of milk accompanied this meal every day. As I said, tea was good, because that was when Father came home.

Sitting at the wooden table, swinging my legs, I'd listen for the sound of his key turning in the lock. Every time I heard it my stomach would flip in excitement. I recall this particular memory so vividly for this was the day my life really began, when I truly started on the road to becoming who I am.

"How's my little boy, then?"

My father had come into the kitchen with a cardboard box, and, after he placed it on the floor, he straightened up and held his arms out to me.

Getting down from my chair I scrambled towards my father. He whirled me round in the air, but my squeals of delight made my mother frown.

"He's been a little shit today, Henry. Ripping shells off snails. There's something wrong with him!" My mother began slamming the masher onto the boiled potatoes—Mother and Father didn't have bread and jam—and she angrily flicked a blob of butter in there and continued her task.

"Peggy, please! Don't say things like that in front of the boy!" My father tickled me under the chin and squeezed me tightly. I remember feeling safe, and knowing that I was his special boy. "Besides, I have a present for someone."

My mother stopped mashing and turned around, her face full of expectation and smiles. Father set me down, and I stood while he knelt beside me, pulling the cardboard box towards us. Mother knelt down also, her anger forgotten, and placed her hand upon Father's knee. He indulged her with a smile and brushed his hand over hers before opening the flaps of the box.

A scratching noise from within made my mother's brow crease and a sigh escaped her pursed lips. "Henry, we discussed…"

"I know, I know, but he needs a playmate!"

Her "tsk!" of disapproval, I recall, made me feel happy inside. The gift within the carton was for me, not her, and it was evident that this upset her.

Father opened the remaining three flaps and reached inside the box. A hiss and a scrabbling noise erupted from the container, which caused my father to jump back. He pulled his hands from the box and immediately sucked at the back of his hand. I watched as blood formed in small beads from three scratches. My mother leapt up to grab a tea towel.

Father's brow furrowed. Mother cautiously turned down the flaps of the box and peered inside.

"It'll have to go back, Henry. I said this was a bad idea." Mother's mouth flattened into an ugly straight line.

"It's afraid, Peggy, that's all." Father patted his hand with the tea towel, and all this time I stood still, wondering what was in the box that could have hurt my father and caused him to bleed. Whatever it was, I had already decided not to like it.

Feeling brave, I inched closer to the box. My hands dove into the carton and I grabbed it. It was a tabby kitten. It didn't hiss nor mew. It dangled; toes splayed, claws out, as I held it aloft. As the kitten looked down at me, I felt rage, proper rage, for the first time.

"You hurt my daddy, you little fucker!" I bellowed loudly.

Father looked at me in complete astonishment. I thought it was because he felt I was his big brave boy for being able to hold the cat without being scratched.

"Where did you hear that word, John?"

Without hesitation, I answered. "Mummy. She called me that today."

I wandered off to the garden with the kitten where I pulled at its ears and tail and pinched the baggy, furry skin on its flank until it mewled quite piteously. I could hear Mother and Father shouting, but paid no heed. My mind was more intent on hurting the kitten and paying it back for scratching my father.

Over the next few years though, that cat brought me gifts that made me extremely happy. I could perform operations on them. I especially liked doing this when they were still alive.

Chapter Two

When you stab a pin in a bird's eye it tends to squawk quite loudly.

***

I named the kitten Twinkle and although I hated him for hurting my father I couldn't help but admire him for becoming my partner in crime.

By age ten, I was a surly looking young boy of stocky build with curly black hair, and a nasty countenance. I didn't have any friends, preferring my own company—and that of Twinkle. And, of course, my father, when he was home.

The cat followed me everywhere and sometimes earned himself a swift kick to his guts for his adoration. Regardless of my treatment of him, at least once a week Twinkle would bring me a gift. A mouse, rat or mole, usually. Mostly these were dead, shaken violently by Twinkle. From the age of seven, I wished I could kill in such a manner, and I would dream of doing just that, waking up in a cold sweat, wearing a big smile on my face.

One of my favourite memories is the day Twinkle brought me a bird, still twittering and flapping. Twinkle sat proudly watching me. I knew my face was wreathed in a smile because my cheeks hurt and I remember my heart pounded so hard that the noise in my ears was almost deafening, and I had butterflies in my stomach.

I sat and held the bird in my hands, holding down its wings, and thought about what I would do to it. The other animals I had just cut up, examining them intently before becoming bored and slinging their bloodied, mangled corpses over the fence into the garden next door. This outraged the neighbour, Mrs Drayton, but I did not care. I developed a sense of isolation from what was morally right the day Twinkle entered my life. If I enjoyed doing something then I did it again. It seemed a very simple and logical thing to me at the time.

I got up, and, holding the bird in one hand, I stole into the kitchen as quietly as I could lest I disturb my mother, who was napping on the sofa. She had taken to having *afternoon drinks* of gin and disappearing upstairs with whoever had rung the doorbell. Mother's behaviour did not bother me, for during such afternoons I bunked off school, hiding in the shed with the spoils Twinkle brought me. I'd while away the hours performing my operations lost in my own demented world.

I took a pincushion, complete with pins and needles, out into the garden shed and, with Twinkle at my heels, we ensconced ourselves in our little den and began the task at hand.

The wren was small and I held it easily in my left hand. In my right, I held a pin between my thumb and forefinger. I teased the bird by looming the pin towards its eye to see if it felt any fear at the small tool in my hand. Its eyes only widened when I squeezed its body quite hard. Although the bird was undoubtedly frightened, I wanted it terrified.

With a quick movement, I plunged the pin into the bird's eyeball and was quite alarmed at the loudness of its squawk. I jumped a little, but regained my composure and pulled the pin out. A clear liquid oozed from the eyeball, and the wren's beak opened and closed as it chirped its protest. I could feel its wings trying to flap within my grip, struggling for freedom, and this made me laugh. Twinkle sat and purred, his wide green gaze never wavering from that bird.

I grinned at Twinkle, and then selected a different needle. So much thicker and longer, I was intrigued to know what would happen when I stabbed a wool needle into my feathered friend's eye.

The force with which I poked must have been too much, and not only did the needle go through the eye and into its head, but out

12

through the other eye, too. The feel of that gooey substance on my fingers from the needle's violent exit excited me, and my penis began to tingle.

That was when my hobby began to get more interesting. Filled with a strange sense of euphoria, I carefully placed the bird under my boot. Twinkle meowed and tossed back his head showing his teeth in what I could only describe as a partner's smile in the bird's death.

The sound of the back door being yanked open startled me.

"John! Are you in the shed with that bloody cat again?" my mother's inebriated voice yelled across the back lawn.

As I left the shed I wiped my hand on my trousers and scraped bird entrails from my boot onto the grass.

"Yes! What do you want?" I was annoyed with her interrupting me when I was having such fun.

We had ceased being civil with one another a long time ago, but kept up a pretence for my father's benefit.

"Get your fucking arse down to the shop and buy me some tonic water. Make yourself bloody useful!"

When I reached the open back door I could hear Mother's slippers slapping the floor as she walked back into the living room. I knew she would fling herself onto the sofa and await my return with her bottle.

Turning to the cat I said, "Another time then, Twinks, hmmm?" I bent down to tickle his head. He raised himself on his hind legs, wrapping himself around my ankles. Lifting him into the air on my foot, I flung him as far as I could, but he landed, as always, on all four paws unharmed. "Fucking cat!"

Taking the money my mother had left on the table, I did as she had bid, taking pleasure when Mr Walker from the shop exclaimed, "What is this red goo stuck to this pound note, boy?"

I shrugged, smiled, and took the change.

"Bird brains, you stupid bastard," I muttered as I left the shop and ran full pelt back home before Mother had reason to hit me.

Chapter Three

Hearing the crack of a fish's spine was maybe one of the best sounds my ears had ever heard. The business of filleting that fish, the gore and the mess that followed, gave my excitement a sharper edge.

***

Many will wonder when they have finished reading my account, why I should have written it in the first place.

Here I sit, with my large notebook and sharpened pencil, looking out at the stream that runs along the edge of my back garden. People like me are misunderstood. Although I have successfully evaded capture for the murders I have committed, I wish to leave this world knowing that my story might possibly help people who read this to understand the reasons *why* I committed such frightful acts.

I realise the average person can't truly understand such reasons, but I hope to convey who I really am inside despite my heinous faults. I mean who people like me really are and the feelings and needs of such a person. What makes me tick.

The trickle of the stream takes me back again to my childhood, to yet another episode, or landmark, if you like, in my life.

I used to fish in this brook with my father. He really was my idol, and I his prince. In my eyes, the sun rose and set with him; he could do no wrong. After all, when my father was home his very presence protected me from my mother.

After I was born, it did not sit well with Mother that she was no longer the sole light of Father's life. With eagerness, she grabbed any opportunity she found to belittle me.

I feel that if she had loved me as much as my father had, maybe I wouldn't have chosen the path that I did of hurting the snails, the birds, and the mice. My frustrations surfaced at a young age, and the only way I could feel better about myself was to hurt something else. In a way, I suppose you could say that the way my mother made me feel was the way I wanted those animals I tortured to feel. To hurt them was to hurt my mother, and to torture them was to pay her back for not loving me.

I knew where I stood with her quite early on. I was to do her errands and keep out of her way the rest of the time. Then I'd snatch my father's attention the minute he was home to hurt her even more.

Fishing with my father at the stream gave us time to share without my mother's presence. I loved these times, and I loved the maggots. I spent many hours squashing them and cutting them in half with my fingernails. My father would sit at the side of the stream, rod in the water, and wait for a bite. Some days he caught nothing at all. Other days he got quite a catch, and we were able to take it home for tea. No bread and butter for me on those nights.

"Hand me a maggot, son."

I looked at my father, already grey at thirty-five. I can't recall him ever being any different. I smiled at him, and, looked into the tin at the squirming maggot bodies, trying to grip one between my finger and thumb. I had to suppress the urge to squeeze each one of them for eluding my grasp.

"Give me the tin, John. We'll be here all day if I leave it to you!"

He ruffled my hair before he took the tin, grinned at me with his overly large teeth, and I felt absurd for having a lump form in my throat. Expertly, my father snagged a maggot on the hook and I watched as he lazily cast off into the water.

"Going to get us a trout, son. I'll teach you how to gut it."

I smiled. Not only was my father spending time with me, but he was also going to show me how to kill a fish.

***

15

In the end, it wasn't a trout, but a bass, and quite large to my eyes, probably around four pounds in weight. I watched as my father unhooked it and laid it on some newspaper he had spread out over the picnic rug. With a quick movement, he took a small wooden cudgel and bopped it on the head. Stunned, the fish then lay quite still. Putting his left palm under the fish's head, Father tilted the head upwards, and, using his cudgel again, gave the fish a sharp crack on the spine.

The cracking of the bones made me feel tingly in my groin, and I sat rapt as I watched him.

"This might not be the right way, John, but it was the way I was taught by my father. You see the belly there?" He produced a sharp flick knife and placed the point of it at the base of the fish's gills, and then looked at me. I smiled and nodded. "Insert the knife through there and slice from gill to tail, fast."

Father did this swiftly, and then raised his knife twice, lopping off the tail and the head.

"You take the head off after the slice, John, to get a clean cut. Now then, do you feel up to cleaning this fish out after I open him up?"

Did I ever! I wish he had told me what he was going to do before he had caught the fish, so that I could have chopped off its head and tail myself. The fish was opened up like a book and I used an old spoon to clean out the intestines and innards. My tongue poked out at the side of my mouth in concentration. I felt so gleeful at the sight of the gore and mess.

"Now then, you see that long bone there, it's called the…"

"Spine."

"Good, lad, the spine. Pull it up from the back, and the skeleton should follow with it."

I dug my fingers at the bone, gripped it and pulled. It made a quiet squelch as it lifted out and I was left looking at raw fish meat.

"We'll leave the skin on. Give the batter something to cling to. How's that sound?" My father was beaming at me, as I was at him. A sense of having shared something together, a man thing, made me feel very proud.

My father turned away, selected another maggot, and hooked it up and cast off. He hoped to catch two more fish, one for each of us.

I got up, walked over to a large tree, and sat with my back against it, facing away from my father. I went over the fish-gutting procedure in my mind, with my eyes closed and my face lifted up to the sun. The lust for doing that task by myself made my penis swell, and I slid my hands into my trousers and fiddled with myself. The feelings produced by my childish fumbling made me feel whole, alive.

At that moment I realised that my true calling was to kill or watch something be killed, to operate on helpless animals, or to gut a numb fish. Yes, that's what I was born to do.

Chapter Four

I overheard two teachers talking once.
"He stares at me whenever I reprimand him. It goes right through
me. It really gives me the creeps."
"I know what you mean, Val, but you've got to bear in mind his
home life. I think anyone would act just like him if they had a mother
like his..."

***

When Father was at work, Mother had her own way of making money.

As I think I said before, when I bunked school I would spend my days in the garden shed, venturing into the house only when I was thirsty or hungry. Mother neither cared nor commented about where I was or what I was doing. She had her own world, her own life that she led that had become far removed from what I remember during my early years.

My father worked many hours trying to "keep our heads above water". Times were hard financially, yet he continued to do his best to provide food and pay the mortgage and bills. He thought Mother worked in a shop. I knew she did not. She would supplement Father's earnings with her "wages", and, looking back, any extra that she made she obviously spent on her gin and bottles of tonic water.

On the days I skipped school, I would stand in the kitchen stuffing bread down my throat, or guzzling a long, cool glass of water and

18

hear my mother and father's bed squeak. Grunts and various hoots of laughter would drift down the stairs. Each day the male voice would be different. Her gin bouts had become longer, one glass turning into many prior to these men's visits.

On one such occasion, the noises I heard were louder than usual, the male voice abrupt, the bed squeaks harsher.

Curiosity got the better of me, even though I had a fair idea of what was happening from the films that I watched long after Mother and Father went to bed. I put my drinking glass in the dishpan as quietly as I could, fearing I would be heard.

I walked to the hallway, taking my cricket bat that was leaning against the wall in hand. The stairs appeared as a mountain, and in my fantasy world, I the mountaineer. Armed with my bat as my crampon, I climbed. My ears pricked to alert mode, I imagined myself as an arctic explorer, and having reached the apex, I had to stalk my prey to give me sustenance for the journey ahead.

Creeping on my toes along the landing, I paused to steady my breathing outside my parents' bedroom door. When I felt ready, when the cries from the room were getting louder, I leaned my bat against the wall and put my hand on the door handle. Turning it, I peeked through the crack in the door.

The images I saw made my penis tingle, just as the gutting of the bass had done. The man was atop my mother, grunting as a pig at a food trough. Fascinating scenes played out before me. My mother was dressed in a school uniform, a short grey skirt that had ridden up and bunched around her waist. Her white blouse was open, revealing her heaving breasts that were spilling out of a black lacy bra. Her head whipped from side to side upon the pillow, her sweat soaked hair flicking through the air and landing across her face.

Her hands gripped the man's buttocks so hard that his flesh poked up between her fingers, and his animalistic grunts reminded me of Twinkle when he caught his prey. The man was holding himself up by his arms, his naked torso away from my mother so he could look down at her in raptures.

I stood transfixed, rooted to the spot if you like, while I watched this act. Images of the girls at school flitted through my mind and I imagined that Mother was one of them and that I was this man. One girl at school, Francesca, particularly caught my attention when I did attend school. Her white ankle socks were her main attraction, her slim calves seeming to grow out of them like flowers from the soil.

My mother opened her eyes and looked up at the man, a laugh exploding from her.

"Have you been a bad girl, Peggy?"

Mother's eyes widened and her mouth formed an "O" shape.

"No, sir, I haven't been bad."

Her voice was childish, not unlike Francesca's. This surprised me, as I hadn't heard her speak like this before. Usually she was sharp and rough when speaking to me, and she hardly uttered a word to my poor father lately.

"Oh, I think you have, young lady!" The man's voice was low and gruff, and my mother let out a pathetic giggle while he still pumped into her.

I wanted to feel what they were feeling, experience what looked to be so thrilling and exciting, so much so that I felt myself straining against my pants. A throbbing had started, my balls were achingly tight, and almost without realising it, I had begun to rub myself through my trousers.

My breaths grew sharp and I feared being heard. Upon reflection, my mother and the man were making too much noise of their own to have heard me, and, eyes like saucers, I continued to watch.

The man seemed to spin my mother round in one fluid motion and onto her front. It was then that I got to have a look at *him*. His member was long and thin, sticking outwards at a right angle, its shaft wet and sticky looking. I remember feeling awe at how long it was, but that I wanted mine to grow thicker and stouter when I was a man.

Thick black hairs covered his legs; his back was like my father's chest, except the hairs were straighter and denser on his shoulder blades. Thighs that were thick and hard with taut muscles appeared as wide to me as tree trunks. His knees seemed to have disappeared into the mattress, his toes splayed like fingers stretched into a star shape.

My mother raised herself onto her hands and knees, and the man seemed to plunge himself into her. Where, at this time in my life, I had no idea, although I did know there was a hole there somewhere.

Films that I watched did not show the opening of a woman, just that the bodies were joined.

He moved rapidly, frantically, and I could watch no more. My own penis was screaming to be touched. I ran to my room on silent feet, and fiddled with myself until I became sore, replaying what I had seen over and over in my mind until my penis bled, which heightened my tingles even more.

Chapter Five

For a child to hate his mother at such a young age is not good. For the mother to cause the father upset is not allowed. To give the child's idol sleepless nights, does not bode well for the future of the mother.

***

Towards the end of my tenth year, I had seen many a maiming of small animals, and many of my mother's sexual encounters.

My father had become somewhat subdued of late; melancholy, depressed, and once I even caught him crying.

"Never be ashamed to cry, John," was all he said on that occasion, wiping away his tears with the back of his hand.

I remember standing as if in shock, my feet planted firmly on the carpet, unable to move. Father's hair seemed a lighter shade of grey, his moustache near white. Thirty-five and old already. His shoulders slumped; he had the air of someone defeated. I know that now, but at the time, I only sensed a change in him.

His shirt, ironed by himself, not my mother, looked worn, and the collar no longer crisp. The centre crease in his trousers had faded on the knees.

I left the room, wondering what had happened to make my father so different. When I had misbehaved in the past, he used to sit me down and talk to me, explain why my misdemeanour was wrong, and ask me what punishment I thought would be fitting for my crime.

The past four months he had taken to striking me, which was a new experience to begin with, but a common occurrence now. Although the smacks hurt, the fact that it was my beloved father hitting me hurt a hundred fold.

Mother had always been the one to reprimand me, so this turnabout had confused me. Mother seemed in a daze half of the time. When the men friends weren't present, she would be surly and walk with an unsteady gait from drinking the gin. When they visited, she would be happy, and the house rang with the sound of her laughter, not to mention the grunts and groans.

On one occasion, I became enlightened as to what ailed my parents. I had been lying in my bed, very nearly asleep when their raised voices disturbed my journey to dreamland. With my eyes still closed, I listened.

"If you weren't such a useless prick, I wouldn't have to do it." Mother's voice was spiteful, and I imagined spittle flying from her mouth as she said this.

"What? I work as hard as I can, earn as much as I can. Why the hell can't you go out to work in a shop like normal women do? Like I was led to believe you were doing!" My father's voice was hoarse, yet firm.

My mother sighed and spoke to my father as if he were a child wearing her patience thin. "Because someone has to be here for John."

The incredulous tone in my father's voice then was evident to me, even as young as I was. "From what I can gather, you spend the whole day on your back, or pissed, and John takes care of himself! What good are you to him? You're not fit to call yourself a mother!"

My mother's voice began to rise as it did when she told me off, and I knew from experience it would raise to a shriek.

"Oh fuck off, Henry. Just fuck off. What the hell do you know anyway?"

I could imagine Mother pacing the carpet now, and I could hear the ice cubes clinking against the sides of her glass. I guessed she was drinking her coveted gin again.

"*Me* fuck off?" My father's barking laughter sounded hollow and frightening to my ears. "It's you who'll be doing that before long!"

The gasp from my mother pierced the blackness around me. I drew the covers further up to my chin, squeezing my eyes shut as shivers beset my body.

"You'd chuck me out when I'm pregnant?"

"Damn right I will. I don't even know if it's mine! In fact, we can be almost certain it isn't!"

"You cheeky bastard!"

The resounding slap flew through my mind, slamming into the back of my skull as a car into a brick wall, causing me to take in such a deep breath that it hurt my throat. I could not believe that my mother had struck my father. I knew what had been going on with all those men, because I had witnessed it. The result was this pregnancy; I wasn't stupid, even if I *was* young.

My fumblings had a new vigour then, as much for pleasure as for comfort, and I would reach into my pants in search of my safety blanket more than ever in the months to come.

***

After I had finally fallen asleep, my parents must have come to some form of stalemate as no men visited my mother—at least none that I ever saw. Soon after, our wealth took a sharp nosedive to say the least. Back to bread and butter, minus the jam. If I thought it had been bad before, it was nothing compared to how we lived now, as Mother didn't get another "job" and stayed at home mainly lounging on the sofa.

Looking back, I was happier when my parents had been arguing, as my father tended to keep away from Mother and chose to spend his evenings with me. The attention I received was wonderful, and the fact that it upset her made it so much better.

Father's attention, however, was now focused on Mother. He spent more time with her, obviously trying to salvage their marriage from the tatters it had become.

Rows still erupted occasionally when my father would come in from work to no meal. I had taken to making my own meal of sorts for myself each day, usually of bread, beans on toast, or a boiled egg if there were any.

"What have you been *doing* all day?" My father wearily put his briefcase down on the cluttered table in the kitchen.

"I'm tired, Henry. This baby is taking it out of me." Mother put on a suitably trite face, as she stood with her hip leaning against the work surface in the kitchen.

"You and me both, Peggy. Don't forget..."

I stood and shuffled my feet as I had been making a sandwich when Father had come in. Mother stood waiting for the kettle to boil. I had yet to be told officially that I had a new sibling on the way, and the shock on my father's face upon seeing me there was highly evident.

"John!" His mouth was agape. "We, uhh, have something to tell you, son."

I wedged some bread into my mouth and mumbled, "I know."

My mother offered a secret smile and turned to make her coffee, leaving Father to explain the mess she had created.

I hated her so much at that moment. I could feel the revulsion rise within me like a tidal wave, engulfing me to the point where I felt I wouldn't be able to breathe if I didn't swallow that hunk of bread. She had hurt my father, and hurting him had hurt me.

Just as Twinkle had hurt him all those years ago, I knew what I had to do to make myself feel better, as I could hardly kill *her*. Shoving past my mother, walking past my father, brushing his sleeve with my arm as I went, I walked out of that house in search of that fucking cat.

Chapter Six

If you tried to place a golf ball in a cat's mouth, forcing it in may well dislocate its jaw, causing the animal to scream in pain. Yet using your father's pliers to remove its teeth makes them pass out.

***

The sun has gone in behind a cloud and my hand is beginning to cramp from this furious writing. This need to write seems to have gripped me like a fever, and now that I have much time on my hands, I suppose I feel that I am using the time I have left wisely. Reliving these experiences, of course, is a pleasure in itself as every memory that I recall takes me back to that place and time.

I can smell the same aromas as I did then. The maggots in the tin could have been on this very table I am leaning on, the images from back then so vivid now.

I should call it a day here and write about my episode with Twinkle tomorrow, but you could say my blood is up and pumping with such force that I know, cramp or not, I shall recount that experience now. Even if my handwriting isn't as legible as it was when I first sat down with my empty notebook.

So much to tell! You may find the stories I have told you chilling, but believe me, you have not read the last of it.

***

When I marched out of that house, fists clenched in temper and determination, I felt ready to explode. I grew more annoyed when the cat didn't come when I called him. Visiting Twinkle's usual haunts in the front garden proved fruitless, and my anger rose to the boiling point.

My father had shouted my name as I left, but he did not follow me. I am sure he had other things on his mind at that moment that took precedence over a sulky ten-year-old boy's feelings. He was right to leave me be. Coming after me would have caused me to utter many a word I would have bitterly regretted.

Mrs Drayton, the neighbour who received my animal carcasses over the fence, puffed out her cheeks at me when I slammed our front garden gate.

"Puff all you want, you old cow," I muttered as I stormed past the garden wall that she was perched upon.

"I beg your pardon, young man?" Her mouth dropped open. She really did seem affronted, but a boy on a mission, and with a grievance in mind, was not one to cross. Not when his name was John Brookes, anyway.

"Fuck off! You heard me." I felt manly swearing at her, my chest visibly swelled, and I turned to scowl at her, staring at her with the eyes that gave my teacher the creeps.

"Oh!" she whimpered, and patted her headscarf that hid the rollers she wore. Her cheeks stained crimson and her mouth looked like a gasping fish.

For a second I felt remorse for speaking to her in this way, but it was only a second, and my mind went back to wondering where in the hell Twinkle was.

I walked once up and down the street before I realized that the cat wasn't going to be found anywhere. I knew he was probably in the shed, but since I walked out of the front door in such a huff, I would feel ridiculous going back through the house again so soon. I would feel silly, and I didn't want to feel like that. I had to mask my inner feelings, that I was just a young boy, confused, wanting a proper family. Deep down I yearned for the three of us to all get along but I didn't entertain those kinds of thoughts very often. They hurt and made me cry.

I turned down an alley between two houses, made my way to the end and turned left. Our back garden was the fourth one along. I used the back gate and quietly gained access to the garden as I heard my parents' voices, loud and sharp, obviously battling out their differences now that they thought I was no longer within earshot.

I ignored what they were saying. I knew my father was hurting; I didn't need confirmation by listening to more.

I passed through the gate and into the garden, making my way towards the shed. My anger had abated somewhat, simmering down to a quiet bubble like a slow cooking stew, but somehow it was more dangerous than my rage upon leaving the house.

I found Twinkle lying on his side on the shed roof, lounging in the sun. Fast asleep, the stupid animal didn't hear my approach until it was too late. I grabbed his fur into my fist, and lifted him from the roof by the scruff of his neck, carrying him into the shed. I kicked the door shut behind me.

***

Inside the shed, I felt calmer. I dropped the cat to the floor while I turned and locked myself in, twisting the flimsy catch to the lock position.

I turned to Twinkle. He sat looking at me in a puzzled manner. If he could have spoken I'm sure he would have asked me if I wanted him to catch a gift.

"What the fuck are you looking at?" I hissed. Twinkle seemed to sense that this wasn't going to be one of my ordinary torture sessions, as his hackles raised. His eyes darted from me, to the door, to the shelves, and, seeing no escape, he took the opportunity to wind himself around my ankles in an attempt to placate me.

I grabbed that cat hard around his middle and began to squeeze; I wanted to literally force his innards out through his mouth, such was my anger. But, I wasn't strong enough. I started to feel panic, and then anger at the panic, and it was then, as I glanced frantically around the shed, that I knew what I was going to do.

My father kept his golf balls in a plastic flowerpot. I took out a ball and sat down on the floor, placing Twinkle between my splayed legs. I drew my knees together, holding the cat between them so that Twinkle faced me. I tried to open his mouth and it was then that he began to struggle, biting down hard on my fingers while at the same time squirming out from between my legs, his claws going in all directions. Gripping him by the scruff of the neck, I tried to shove the golf ball into his mouth but that cat was too strong, too angry and he scratched at me, drawing blood.

Gazing around the shed, I began to look on the shelves to see what I could use to inflict misery on Twinkle. The yowls he was making didn't seem to be enough for me. I wanted that cat squealing like a stuck pig. I imagined those cries of distress as my mother's.

My gaze landed on a pair of my father's pliers and I jumped up to get them. Twinkle scrabbled to the door, frantically scratching at it to get out and away from me. With the adrenaline coursing through me, I felt he wouldn't get the better of me now. I'd expected a few scratches and the prospect of more didn't faze me.

The pliers felt heavy in my hand, yet opening and closing them showed me that they were easy to operate. At first, it went through my mind to cut sections of Twinkle's tail off, bit by bit. But upon watching the cat manically darting from one side of the shed to the other I saw that his lips were drawn back from his teeth, and that was what gave me the idea.

Again gripping the cat by the scruff, I sat down on the dusty shed floor and resumed the same position I had been in before. He fought like a wild thing and his claws found my face. Still trying to grasp the cat by the neck with one hand while gripping his front paws with the other, I held his head as steady as I could between my legs despite his thrashing around. Then, picking up the pliers with my right hand, I realised I couldn't pull his teeth out as I had planned, so I bashed at them instead.

It wasn't until the cat passed out from the sheer pain of it all that I let him go, tossing him across the shed like so much refuse. My anger at my mother at last began to abate.

His body looked sunken. His mouth a hideous mess, lips drawn back, gums bleeding, his fur streaked with red.

I didn't feel an ounce of remorse, but a sense of well being. Harming Twinkle had so easily sated the terrible anger that had raged within just moments before. I can't explain why I didn't feel it was wrong. Oh, I knew people *said* this kind of behaviour was very wrong, indeed, but as it didn't feel that way, I decided to always go with my instincts, and do whatever my mind and body instructed.

Chapter Seven

A baby being born is usually a joyous occasion within a family. However, for us, it was not.

***

I finally had to give in last night, wrap things up and run a bath, read over what I'd written. What I've written so far may not make sense, and that is the last thing I want. I need any future readers of this to understand me. This is very important to me.

A new day. A new page. Writing this now, my hand spasmed slightly at having to write again but I'm sure I'll get used to it.

Today, I am lying on my sun lounger, the head end propped to a comfortable sitting position, a pillow upon my lap on which my note book is resting on my bended knees.

It looks like it will be a hot day. The sun baking everything reminds me of the day we moved from Churchill Street and into the cabin.

Mother had gone into the hospital to have the baby a few days previously, and when it had been born I remember my father coming home looking utterly at a loss.

"She's had it, then?" A question I didn't need to ask, but I didn't quite know what else to say.

"Yes, John. She's had it." He sighed, a deep exhalation that had him blowing the air from his mouth through pursed lips, as if he were going to whistle.

He sat on the edge of the sofa, legs bent, elbows resting on his knees, fingers rubbing his eyes so viciously I'm surprised he didn't push his eyeballs into the back of his head.

Again, not knowing what to say, I managed, "What did she have?"

Letting his hands flop between his open knees my father looked at me with red rimmed, blood shot eyes. "A boy, John. A boy."

"When will she be bringing it home?"

"I don't know, and I don't care." He took a deep breath. "I know you don't understand, being only eleven and all, but that baby is no son of mine. It's just you and me now, kid."

A surge of elation swam through my veins; did I dare hope that he meant what he said? That it was just him and me? That Mother wasn't coming back with a squalling brat half-brother in tow?

"What d'you mean, Dad?"

"Just what I said, John. We'll be moving into the cabin where we go fishing. I'll rent it out for the two of us, and the place should suit us nicely. Take Twinkle with us, mind you."

Twinkle had got over being toothless quite quickly. Mother and Father, with their own problems to deal with, had barely taken the time to wonder why the family cat was walking round without any teeth.

The cat had taken to following me around again, more so than before, and despite me kicking him repeatedly, he apparently adored me. I found it quite bizarre that an abused animal trusts and follows its abuser. I thought this quirk fascinating and vowed to look into this kind of thing when I became a man. I mused that I might even become a famous animal psychologist or a veterinary surgeon. But you had to have a good education for that so either I buckled down at school, or scrapped that idea completely.

So, it came to pass that we moved from Churchill Street into the cabin, taking only what was necessary. As Mother was to stay in the hospital for at least ten days, due to having a difficult birth and a Caesarean section, Father put the house up for sale and explained to me that Mother could live there until it was sold. We wouldn't be going back, he said. I, however, had other ideas on that score.

The cabin had two bedrooms, a living area, kitchen and bathroom. It was ample space for Father and me, and I felt at last that my life was going to run smoothly. I decided to attend school, to try and get along and actually learn something. Make my father proud of his only son.

The rent was low, due to repairs that needed doing on the property. Father assured the landlord he would carry these out himself, so long as the rent stayed at its reasonable price.

I figured the winters would be cold, only having the one fireplace in the main living area, but I was a strong boy and told myself we would cope with anything, so long as we had each other. That was all that mattered.

How did I feel that first week at the cabin? Free and easy, safe and wanted, special and loved. Father had the week off from work, and he fixed tiles on the roof, holes in the walls, and put cupboard doors back on their hinges. It was a busy seven days, and I suspect Father enjoyed it as much as me, and that it took his mind off of the traumas he had experienced of late.

The cabin wasn't as you would imagine, made of logs and such. I have no idea why it was called a cabin, except the round plaque on the wall beside the front door proclaimed it as such. Constructed of the common house brick, it offered a cosy retreat for us both. A place to lick our wounds and start afresh, creating an even stronger bond than had previously existed between us.

Chapter Eight

Seeing Mother again had the blood in my veins pumping. I had to hold myself in check. Had I followed my gut instinct, she would have been prostrate upon the ground within a second, and my boot would have smashed her features like nothing more than a cookie beneath my tread.

***

Two weeks later. I saw my mother walking down High Street, pushing a pram. She did not see me and I was able to follow her relatively easily.

She looked tired, a few grey hairs had appeared amongst the brown and she had clipped it back with a hair band. Her face was pinched, her walk unsteady and slow. I guess the operation scars were still healing, and I remembered hoping she was in some considerable pain. I wished that by bringing her child into the world she would forever be plagued by discomfort and unhappiness for the rest of her days. I wanted her to pay for the pain and unhappiness she had caused my father and me all these years.

The pram she steered was mine, which of course caused me immense anger, mixed with jealousy that this brat was sleeping in something I had once slumbered in myself. It was a Silver Cross that bounced on its wheels, and had a wide comfortable carriage.

I trailed her through the town and its shops, watched what she bought. It looked to me that she didn't buy very much; maybe the shape of a milk carton was evident through the carrier bag she placed in the pram's basket. I noted that she left the pram and its contents outside each shop that she visited. As she left town, I pursued her to where she now lived. It was not Churchill Street, but Wrathmore Road, aptly named I felt. I would come here again tomorrow, early, and watch the house. I had an insane urge to learn her movements. Besides, I had a half brother I wanted to meet.

***

That afternoon I went back to the house in Churchill Street. It was still up for sale, no reason for Mother to move out so soon, but she had, and this gave me a place to go this boring Saturday.

Amazingly, the key was still hanging by its string on the inside of the door, easily accessed via the letterbox. Thinking about that now, I am amazed that it was left so carelessly, but at the time, it was only natural that the feel of the string should be there when I waggled my fingers through that letterbox.

Letting myself in, I wandered through the house, still with many of our belongings in it from when we lived there. Of course, the three-piece suite we had in the cabin, but the large dresser that ran along one wall in the living room was still there, looking huge and majestic without anything else in the room.

Father had taken a few items from it, a couple of picture frames and a brass bird—a starling—but everything else remained on display behind the glass doors. Mother obviously didn't want anything in it.

The kitchen table still stood, wood scarred from my stabbing it with a fork at meal times when I didn't want my food. Even a groove was cut out of the side where I had sawed it with my knife.

At eleven-years-old, it was difficult to stand there and take it all in, that we no longer lived as a threesome. That we had all branched out and separated. Only a quick fleeting thought on that subject before I told myself it was better this way. And yes, it really was. My life was more ordered. I knew what was coming, yet I still carried within me this enormous hate for my mother that I knew would one day rage out of control. Why couldn't she just love me like a mother should? That's all she had to do and everything would have been okay.

The shed was full of so many memories it actually brought tears to my eyes, especially when I saw the brown blood stain on the wooden floor where Twinkle had so recently lay unconscious, bleeding from the gums. The smell in there gave me a sense of security, and I wished I could somehow take the building back to the garden at the cabin. Of course, I couldn't, and it was the only thing from Churchill Street that I was sad to leave behind.

***

Sunday morning dawned bright and warm. I packed my rucksack with some water in an old pop bottle, and a sandwich, knowing Father would be fishing in the stream that ran along the edge of our garden.

"You off for the day, son?" Father turned his head towards me, as I made my way round the side of the cabin.

"Yes. Going to go and play at the park." I had to squint as the sun was in my eyes.

"Good lad." His hand gave a quick wave.

Father resumed his study of the opposite bank, and I checked the contents of my bag. I had a busy day planned.

Mother came out of the house on Wrathmore Road around ten a.m., strolling slowly with her brat in the pram. I wished I were the baby in the pram that she was pushing along. I saw that her hips didn't sway as they once did; her legs seemed stiff and straight, as if her knees could no longer bend. Staying a little way behind, I followed her.

I felt like I was a detective, Sherlock Holmes as I recall, and then discarded that idea for being a stalker instead. She looked a little better in the face today. Maybe she'd had a night of undisturbed sleep, who knew? But she did look more refreshed, her cheeks rosy and shining from a recent wash.

We walked for a while, her in front, me behind, and I waited down the side of the small newsagents that we had come to as she put the brake on the pram and went inside the shop, leaving the baby outside.

I do not know where the idea had come from, how it had got into my head or when, but at that moment, when I walked up to that pram and looked inside, the reality and certainty of what I was about to do was born.

Chapter Nine

The baby lay sleeping in the pram. Button nose, rose bud lips, and a quiff of hair like Elvis Presley. Skin that felt like a peach, and dark lashes that rested upon the tops of his cheeks as softly as a butterfly on a petal.

***

Lifting that bundle out of the pram as carefully as I could lest it cry, I clasped it to my chest and began to walk quickly away from the shop towards Churchill Street. The baby made not a whimper, still fast asleep, swaddled tightly in a knitted white blanket like a caterpillar in a cocoon.

I walked through the back gate once I had arrived at the house, and inside via the back door, which I had left unlocked on my last visit.

I stepped into the living room and placed the bundle down on the carpet and knelt, resting on my haunches to inspect this child that was related to me.

Unwrapping the blanket, the baby's arms flung outwards in a reflex action, and as it was still asleep, I was able to study it to my heart's content.

Its face was that of my mother's, albeit in a smaller form, its hair brown like hers. It was easy to imagine this baby as her, and any guilt in stealing this child that may have surfaced in someone else did not bother me at that time.

I began to undress it with considerable care. I did not want it waking up at this stage. The air, though, must have chilled this now naked being, as it was then that his eyes opened widely, his mouth formed a large circle, and he began to scream.

I panicked, not knowing how I would shut it up. I raced to close the curtains, my bowels threatening to lose their contents. Why I was so scared I do not know. I was usually fearless. Maybe deep down I knew what I was doing was terribly wrong, but on the surface, I did not care. Calming myself, I breathed slowly, concentrating. It was then that the idea came to me.

Dressing my brother, albeit awkwardly, I wrapped him up again. He quietened, and, as I had seen on the television, I walked up and down the living room with him in my arms, pacing and rocking until he went back to sleep.

I imagined what Mother would be doing now. Would she be frantically screaming that her baby was gone, had been taken? Would she have rung the police, the shop owner comforting her until the panda car with its blue flashing lights came to her rescue?

I suspect she would revel in the attention, saw, in my mind, a sturdy arm placed along her shoulders, a hand patting the top of her arm. Those policemen, they would murmur that it would be okay. They would find her baby. Come on now, Mrs. Brookes. Calm down, just calm down.

Looking down at the little child, I wondered then if Mother ever did this with me. If I had been wrapped up in a blanket and treated as nicely as this baby evidently had been. It was certainly clean and appeared cared for.

No. I decided she had hated me from the first, had left me squealing in hunger, fists balled, face red with anger, a lonely child who only gained comfort from his doting Father.

Even now I often wonder if Mother had in fact hated that little baby as much as she had me. After all, wasn't he the reason Mother and Father had parted ways? Or maybe she felt that their marriage had crumbled because of me. Yes, that was probably what her warped mind had reasoned, that until I had come along she'd been the centre of attention and everything had been fine. I often wonder why she just didn't abort me. It was obvious I was a burden, a nuisance.

Perhaps she herself had had a terrible childhood and hadn't experienced love from *her* parents, then my father had arrived in her life as a breath of fresh air and she felt loved and wanted for the first time. Had I spoiled it all for her?

I would never know the truth. I'd never found out just what her life had been like as a child. She wasn't one for conversing with me, preferring to shun me, blame me, and make me feel as *she* possibly did in her youth, wanting to inflict upon me what she herself may have endured.

Or, did she feel the baby was all she had in the world? That her husband no longer loved her as he once had, and it was she and the baby against the world. Had she woken up from a drunken stupor and realised how selfish she had been, deciding to turn over the proverbial new leaf? Who knew?

I didn't then, and I don't now.

The decision wasn't consciously made that day. I just did what I did without forming a plan of any kind. The thought of this child being loved and treated properly by Mother must have been too much to bear for I left the house via the back door, baby swaddled against me, and walked.

The light was fading. I must have been in the house for quite some time, and I wondered why the baby still slept, why it hadn't woken expecting a bottle of milk. Maybe my pacing had lulled him into a deep sleep, deeper than usual.

And I walked, kept walking until the sting of the canal assaulted my nostrils and the noise of it gushed into my brain.

The baby started to stir. Wiggling inside the blanket, he strained against my grip and his eyes opened wide, face contorting. He screamed. And screamed. He kept screaming as I ran towards the water.

The noise was so piercing it hurt my head. I stood by the side of the canal, looked left, looked right. No barges. No people.

I took the blanket off my brother, whose arms were flailing, mouth squawking its hunger. I balled one end of the blanket, stuffing it into my pocket, the rest of it trailing beside me in the mud.

There was silence for two seconds while the baby inhaled a deep breath and I took that opportunity to drop it into that canal. It must have plunged like a stone, for I stood for a full five minutes afterwards and he never bobbed to the surface. If Mother couldn't love me, then she couldn't love the baby either.

No remorse, then. None whatsoever.

And the blanket? I don't recall what happened to it.

Chapter Ten

However abhorrent the subject, it is human nature to be curious. Sheer nosiness prods us into wanting *more, even if it does make us a little sick. Does that make me different to you? Are you any less sadistic than I? You are reading about it. I have done it. Are we* really *any different?*

***

I *know!* I killed a baby when I was just eleven-years-old, and I know you are possibly sick to the stomach by now. But aren't you just a little bit curious as to what on Earth I did next? Or what I did about the mud on my shoes from my trip to the canal? Of course you are. This is why you will continue to read.

My mud-stained shoes were easily cleaned. Father was no longer fishing in the stream when I got back, and, making my way down the side of the cabin I ran the length of the garden and found a shallow area of the water and stepped right in.

Using a stone to rub my beige suede shoes, I scrubbed them well. I left them at the back door. It being a warm night they would probably dry by morning.

Taking off my socks, I entered the cabin and hung them over the back of a dining chair.

A crackling noise made me jump. I looked up and spun round to face the living area, to see Mrs Drayton, of all people, sitting on our sofa. The noise was her scrunching up a Murray Mint wrapper after she had popped the sweet into her lipsticked mouth.

"Hello, John."

I was puzzled for a moment. Had she come to tell Father that she had seen and heard me with the baby? More to the point, where was my father?

"Where's my dad?" I glared at her. I knew my eyes were piercing, as I had been practising this look in front of the bathroom mirror. Even I thought I looked scary!

"Sit down, John." She moved the mint around in her mouth, and I heard it bump into her teeth.

"No. Not till you tell me where my dad is." I scowled again, and she shifted in her seat a little, making out she was getting more comfortable, but I knew, oh yes, I knew she was scared of me. And the knowledge felt good.

"Sit down, lad, and I'll tell you." She attempted to smile, her bright pink lips quickly stretching and relaxing again.

I sat.

"Your dad had the police contact me, asking if I'd look after you while he's at the police station. There's been an..." She glanced round the room, then up at the ceiling, obviously trying to find the right words to say. "Occurrence."

What a perfect word selection. It gave me my opportunity to jump up and shout, "An occurrence? Is my dad all right? He was fishing by the stream...did he...fall in or something?"

I stood in front of her, my face set in panic, and I let this scenario run through my mind, imagined my father falling into the stream and banging his head on a rock, and him dying, leaving me alone in the world. The tears fell without much effort. I of course knew exactly what occurrence she was talking about.

"No, John. Your father's fine, love. Come and sit here." She patted the seat next to her, and I heard her loudly swallow the spittle in her mouth.

I sat, again, crying for all I was worth.

She began again, patting me on the back as she said, "Someone stole your mum's baby, John. Took it away, back to your old house.

The police thought it was your dad, love. They came to ask him to go to the Station, he needed…"

"No! My dad wouldn't have done that! I don't believe you!" I turned to her with a suitably horror struck expression, my cheeks were probably bright red and already wet with tears.

"No, no, I know he wouldn't have done that, John. Your dad's a good man. No, he went down to sign a statement. He didn't do it John, because you know the Landlord?"

I nodded, head bent down, looking at the carpet. I saw an earwig making its way over the rough pile and stifled the urge to stamp on it.

"Well, he came over to collect the rent from your dad and spent some time fishing with him. It was very lucky that it was at the time your brother was taken."

I felt at that time that I wanted to shout into her face that the baby wasn't my brother, that he had nothing whatsoever to do with me, but I stopped the words from even forming. I felt sick inside, as I thought my actions had got my father in serious trouble. It was an immense relief that he was not.

"So," she continued. "They know it wasn't your dad, John. They just needed him to go and sign a bit of paper, stating what he was doing and who he was with. That's all. He'll be home shortly, love, and then I can go home. Sorry it's me you're stuck with, but your dad thought of me, and here I am. Now then, would you like a bit of something to eat?"

I thought of what I had eaten that day, which was several hours ago, and I realised I was starting to feel a little hungry. I nodded, and she went off into the kitchen.

It struck me as odd that someone I had been rude to while living in Churchill Street, someone who I undoubtedly annoyed, would have come here at a moment's notice, to look after me while my father was at the Station. I mused that some people were indeed too soft for their own good, but I felt a little respect start to grow inside me for this woman. Sixty if she was a day, putting old grudges aside when someone was in need. I bet she loved *her* children.

I decided that I liked Mrs Drayton.

I got up and followed her to the kitchen.

"Did you ring the police then? Did you see them take the baby next door?"

She turned from the cooker, where she was frying some eggs and bacon. "No, love. I'd only just got back from my daughter's when the police came to ask me if I'd seen anyone going into your old house, and if I would mind coming here to look after you."

She smiled at me, and then looked back at the frying pan, splashing hot oil over the yolks of the eggs. She lifted the food out and put it on a plate. Turning with the plate, she continued talking as she walked into the dining room, and I followed, listening to her prattle on.

"Turns out that the neighbours on the other side were out all day too, and the people opposite are on holiday for the week. No one seems to have seen anything at all. Such a shame, poor baby. Still…"

I cut her off as I sat down to eat. Ramming a whole bacon rasher into my mouth, I quickly chewed and swallowed, then said, "What do you mean, poor baby. You only said someone took it back to my old house…"

"Oh!" Her cheeks went red and her hand flew up to her mouth to cover her quivering lips. "I'll let your dad tell you the rest, love, it's only right."

She turned and bustled back into the kitchen, where she busied herself with washing the dishes. I could hear them clinking around in the dishpan and the occasional sploshing of water.

Chapter Eleven

Time passes in a haze. I suppose I could be classed as semi-normal at this time, but only I knew that lava was boiling beneath the surface, waiting to erupt once again.

***

The next four years moved swiftly by. I still killed things, of course I did, but I had gone back to just animals. Twinkle still at my heels, I spent those years operating on the cat's gifts. Although toothless, the cat was still able to hunt and eat.

Then one day I called Twinkle and he didn't come. Later that afternoon I had been messing about near the stream when I found him. I'd been throwing pebbles into the water, trying to make the biggest splash I could when I noticed his wet and bedraggled body on the other side of the stream.

He had obviously tried to jump from one bank to the other and had fallen in. Had maybe tried to scramble out of the water but only managed to haul himself up the bank a small way before he slumped down and died.

I remember standing staring at that cat, telling myself it couldn't be him, that it was some other moggy. But it wasn't, and I slumped down on the bank and thought of all the times that cat had followed me, how he'd been my faithful friend despite my rounds of cruelty to him. How terribly I had treated him, and still he hadn't minded, adored me despite it all.

To lose him like that…I can't write about him anymore.

Father had been cleared of any involvement in that baby's disappearance. The newspapers and local newsreaders shouted out the heinous crime, but after a week it was everyone's fish and chip wrappers.

My mother didn't call at the cabin after the occurrence. The house on Churchill Street sold, and we moved on with our lives. I did buckle down at school, surprising my teachers, and even myself. I became a veritable sponge, soaking up information. I got good grades, worked hard, and appeared "normal" if there were such a thing.

I still spied on my mother. I spent at least one evening a week after school watching her in her kitchen at Wrathmore Road, washing up or preparing a meal.

She had cut her hair short, almost into a soldier's crop, and now *did* work in a shop, as she should have done all those years ago. From my vantage point, in a tree opposite her house, I saw she still supplemented her income with her prostitute ways, and more than once, I saw her swig gin straight from the bottle. She would get it out of her apron pocket while facing the window at the sink, and neck it back, sometimes shaking her head after she swallowed. I felt nothing but hatred when I saw her, but it didn't make me feel vengeful as it did all those years ago. I was able to control it then, as if God or Destiny had her fate on hold, and that when the time came, I would know when to act upon it.

I revelled in the fact that my mother had effectively lost of both her sons and her husband, because of her jealousy towards me and her whoring actions. I got great satisfaction that Father and I had one another, that we got along tremendously, and he had worked out a niche for himself in life in which he sat comfortably. He was a happy man, content with his job, his home life, and of course, his fishing.

I was a tall lad now, nearly six feet, with broad shoulders and a barrel of a chest. I looked like a grown man, and I remember on my fifteenth Christmas, fiddling with myself while waiting for Father to awake so we could open our presents, that I had indeed got that thick long penis I had so wished for.

That Christmas it all started again. I imagined God began His calling of me, and instructed, in his own mysterious way, that I had another big mission to complete. It *had* to be God talking to me. In our religious studies at school, our teacher told us that God spoke to us, helped us when we needed it. And I needed help, didn't I? Needed someone to show me the way. After reading parts of the bible in class, I fancied myself as one of the chosen ones. Someone who carried out God's instructions. It made me feel good, special.

I did not visit the Church, nor did I practise any religious studies other than at school, nor did I ever pray. I did not need to, as I was special. God spoke to me and showed me signs that only I would recognise. His voice was my instincts and my inner voice.

I was eager to do His bidding.

***

That Christmas, Father bought me a pair of binoculars. I was overjoyed with them. I recall hugging him so hard, almost squashing him as he shyly hugged me back. I ran out into the back garden to test them.

It seemed like I could see for miles—and the detail! Well, to see something that was so far away as if it were right before my very eyes enthralled me, and I spent most of that Christmas holiday with them glued to my eyes.

I have never had a better present, and I still own them even now. They are scuffed, with the hanging strap fluffy in places from over use, yet I can still imagine them as they were the first time I saw them. How shiny they were, dark grey in colour, the strap black, the eyepieces silver. They smelled of brand newness. I can smell it now as I sniff the air, and I smile. What a memory!

On Boxing Day, I was sitting on the back doorstep, peering down at the bushes that dotted the bank of the stream. I had caught a glimpse of a bird going to its nest there, and as I watched it through my binoculars, I wished Twinkle had been there to see it too.

I imagined the cat walking in my line of vision, stalking low in the long grass, towards the hedge. It was a large blackbird, and I sat intently watching, anticipating Twinkle's ghost catching it for me, and the later operation.

48

So I did not hear the stiletto heels clipping down the side of the cabin. I did not hear them stop abruptly a pace away from me. It was the clearing of a throat that alerted me to the presence, and even then, I didn't see who was standing there until I took the binoculars from my eyes and looked up.

She seemed the same, but of course different. I hadn't seen her close up since I was little, but even had I not been spying on her, I would have known her instantly.

"Hello, John." She smiled as if she were the kindest mother in the world, and for a moment, I imagined she was, but memories from childhood flitted through my mind. My rage started to bubble.

I stood up to my full height, expanding my chest and hung my arms down at my sides.

"Is your dad in?" she asked.

Chapter Twelve

Some people do not know when they are better off. Some people just have to re-appear. Those people have to learn that they cannot just swan back into your life and expect to take up where they left off. Some people...

***

I didn't want to speak to her, didn't even want to associate with her, but I did, just the same. Maybe deep down I wondered if she would love me now.

"No. He's out at the pub." I felt the least I said the better.

"Know when he's coming home?"

She spoke to me as if I had only seen her yesterday. I turned and walked into the kitchen, and she had the gall to follow me. She leaned her hip against the doorjamb, her left knee bent, showing an expanse of leg through the slit in her long black skirt. She cocked her head, her stupid short, curly hair bobbing as she did so, and smiled.

"No."

I didn't look at her when I spoke, but began tidying up the kitchen worktops for something to do.

"My," she said, her voice full of wonder as she used her hip to push away from the doorjamb; she then stepped over to me, "You've grown into a fine young man."

She started to touch my arm, but I moved out of her reach. Her hand came towards my binoculars, and I recall feeling a kind of panic mixed with ire, that she, *she* would *dare* touch my beloved binoculars.

I swatted her hand away from them, and to my utter shock, disgust and horror, she clasped my groin in her hand and began to knead.

"A fine young man."

It was absolutely one time in my life where everything she had ever done to me played in my head like a lightning fast cine film. In the second that she had touched me, I saw parts of my life fly through my head, and in the second that followed, I had the point of a knife touching the flesh beneath her chin.

Her hand dropped back to her side, her eyes wide with terror, her sultry act disintegrating.

"Don't fucking touch me. You will *never* fucking touch me again."

She stepped back slightly, causing the knife to prick her skin, drawing blood. I slowly took the knife away, holding it pointing towards her, yet at my side.

"Get out. And never, *ever* come back."

I could have laughed at that point, as she looked so scared that I wouldn't have been surprised if she had shit herself. Walking backwards, still maintaining eye contact, she made her way to the back door, and only when she reached it did she turn and flee. As she passed the kitchen window, I saw her lift her hand to cover her mouth and heard a stifled sob.

Stupid woman. She should have left me alone.

***

My eyes are tired. I have sat up well into the night yet again, scribbling onto this pad as if in a frenzy, wanting to get it all out in case it slips away like mist.

I make my way to my room, undress, and climb into bed, propping my pillows up against the headboard, bending my knees to have something to lean my writing pad on.

My head feels fuzzy at remembering the encounter with my mother. I did not tell my father that she had called round, wanting to shield him from it, as I was sure it would taint his now serene life, and I did not want to spoil that by causing him any pain.

Looking back, what I did next was inevitable. The chain of events that followed Mother's visit was God's instruction, and there was no way I was going to ignore Him.

My mind clears now and becomes sharp. I recall just what I *did* do next. The excitement begins building within me and I feel fully awake, knowing that I will jangle for you now, those very chains of events that followed that stupid woman's visit.

Chapter Thirteen

Those binoculars served me well at that point in my life. In fact, they served me well on several occasions. Mother had tried to touch them, to sully something precious that my father had given me, and then, she touched me. I could not let her go unpunished.

***

I followed her home. I watched her through my binoculars from my vantage point in a tree across the road from her house. She sat at a scarred wooden kitchen table, head upon her folded arms, looking towards me. I could see her as if I was right there in the room, sitting nose to nose with her. If she'd stayed in that position for a long time, I could have counted the pores on her face. I saw the downy hairs, the colour of soft gold that grew along her jaw. I was that close, yet she was not aware.

She looked worn out, defeated and I was glad. I was happy to see her looking dejected, slumped there in her squalid, foetid house. Did seeing me again bring her down? I know it did, as I witnessed a screaming match between her and one of her customers, and watched as she struck him on the face, venting her anger upon him. I saw the rage cross his features as he stalked from her kitchen, from her house, and her life. I sympathised with him, yet at the same time, I was happy that he had left, that she would no longer be in his world.

Her cheeks were red from temper, or the exertion of moving as swiftly as she did when she'd struck him. I hated the way her face turned mottled like that. I detested the grease that lined the roots of her hair. I abhorred the fact that she looked so unkempt. Yes, I knew what she thought when she looked at me on Boxing Day. That I was just a young man and not her son. That she could touch me like she would fruit from a stall, to be felt for its ripeness.

I am fully aware, having watched her every week for nearly five years, and remembering how she acted when she lived with us, that she thought she was above everyone else. Everyone else, however, did not see what I saw.

I had followed her around the front facing rooms of her house each day for the past week. Mostly she just sprawled out on her bed with her male "friends", shovelling dick after dick into her slack, wet mouth. She looked gross when she did that. The scenes made my stomach churn. But I watched her all the same. It fuelled my hatred.

When she lived with us at the house in Churchill Street, she looked at me and said, "You're a little bastard!" each day of my younger years. And every time I said, "I know," even though the words felt like they would strangle me. My mind told me to ignore her, just the once, to see what her reaction would be. I knew what that reaction would be. And as always, she gave me a smack or spouted verbal abuse into my face.

I recalled then the small book of poems Father had bought me when I was around nine-years-old. Whenever I began to read the words, I was transported into another world free from Mother. I could imagine the places described, become the people in the poems. I used it as a form of escape, and when she spat her vile words at me, I would go to my room and open the book of poetry.

One day, she caught me reading that book, and had laughed.

"You're nothing but a fucking pansy boy! Only soft boys read poetry!" Her face was hard as she looked at the book clutched in my hands, and I felt panic that she would try to wrestle it from me, rip out the pages, but she didn't. She stalked from my room, but many times in the future she would spitefully refer to my love of poetry.

Was she aware that I tolerated her when I was young until I was old enough to teach her a lesson? I wished her dead. Yet in reality, there she still was, head lying prone across the tabletop, tears coursing down her face. I did not feel sympathy, just disgust and revulsion.

If I let her, she could have made me physically sick. Over the years, this feeling grew to massive proportions, and no one would ever have known, except maybe Mother herself.

As I sat in the tree opposite her house, watching through my binoculars, she lifted her head, so my dreams of torturing her were put on hold. A woman, who I presume Mother shared her house and her profession with, stepped into the kitchen. I watched Mother turn to her, hastily swiping at the tears she did not wish her friend to see. If she saw them, she might have understood Mother was human after all, that she did have a heart. But her spiteful pride was in the way; she would not allow her friend to see her as anything but poised.

With a snarl on her face, Mother raised her sinful body from the chair and pointed at the woman. Did she not see what I saw? The fear upon her face, the terror Mother inspired in her? Of course she did. It pleased my mother.

The woman left the room, slamming the door, and Mother walked to the sink that faced me and looked out of the window. She couldn't see me sitting in my tree, looking at her from my leafy vantage point. Yet it seemed she was looking right at me. My stomach churned as I wondered if she could *indeed* see me, that the checks I had made into my visibility were wrong. But no, she grasped the kettle handle, and began to fill it with water. Placing it on its stand to boil, she then lit one of her many cigarettes, and slung a gulp of gin down her throat.

The woman had gone outside to calm down, stalking down the road at quite a pace. Mother stood watching her with a look of sheer unhappiness on her face. I had no pity. I looked at her more closely. Sweat beaded upon her upper lip, and across the bridge of her nose, tiny balls balanced with the pores as their anchor point.

Mother filled her glass again and took a large knife from the counter-top. Sitting down at her table she tossed the drink back once more, squeezing her eyes shut as the liquid burned. And then she began toying with the knife.

She ran the blade up and down the inside of her arm and I sat, mesmerised at what she was doing. Fresh tears spilled but she left them unchecked. When she placed the knife, sharpest side down across her wrist, I decided it was time to pay her a visit.

Scrambling down from the tree my jeans got caught on a branch and I frantically tried to shake it free while turning to look through my binoculars at Mother. She appeared to be holding the knife tightly by the handle while pressing down on her wrist in almost jab-like motions. I wanted to be there to watch her do it.

With my leg finally free, I climbed down. Running across the small field where the tree grew, my chest burned as the adrenaline pumped so fiercely that I feared I would lose my breath. I had to get there in time. I *had* to!

I checked for witnesses as I ran into Wrathmore Road and seeing no one, I dashed down the side of Mother's house, into the back garden, hoping, *praying* that there was some way I could get into the property. And God was on my side once more as the back door opened when I turned the handle. The door opened quietly, so I know I hadn't alerted Mother of my presence. Guessing the layout of the house I walked through the lounge and into a hallway. I spotted another door leading off it. It was open and stepping into the doorway, I could see the back of Mother's head, her short curls bobbing as she cried. And she *was* crying. Loud, wracking sobs that made her shoulders shudder.

"Go on. Do it," I said.

I heard her intake of breath, saw her head snap up. I am positive I heard her neck pop. Her head moved round slowly, like it was rolling on casters. A smile twitched her lips.

"You want me to do it, John? You'd stand and watch your mother slit her wrists?"

Was it truly what I wanted? Was it *really*? Could I let her do *that*? She was my mother, and I knew she didn't love me, but...

"Do the world a favour and just do it." Did I mean that? I felt confused, and I wasn't sure what I wanted any more.

I moved to the table, and stood to her right, watching as she continued trailing the knife back and forth across her wrists, which had become red as if chafed, the blade not doing any damage at all. I didn't think she had enough courage to actually harm herself.

"You'd like that, wouldn't you, John? Just as you liked having your father all to yourself. You know, before *you* came along, my life was wonderful. How you *ruined* it. I've never forgiven you for that."

She smiled her secret smile again, the one I recall from my earlier years yet this time it was somehow tinged with sadness.

"Didn't you love me at *all*?" I don't know why I asked her that, it just came out and I felt angry with myself for showing her my weakness, letting her know she had something over me.

She sighed, pressed harder with the knife. "Oh, for a little while, yes, I think I did. But you were too cute, too cuddly, and your father just couldn't resist lavishing you with attention, leaving me feeling left out!" With those last few words, she stabbed at her wrists with the point of the knife, and blood dripped from her arm onto the tabletop.

Her words left me feeling hollow, and I felt my anger returning. It came rushing at me with the force of a broken dam.

"You're doing it the wrong way, you silly bitch. You see, I learned more than you thought at school. Biology was my favourite lesson and when I studied, I studied well." I remember my face felt hot, my jawbone pulsed as I grit my teeth and I wanted to wring my mother's neck. But I didn't.

"Well now, John, and there was me thinking I'd given birth to a retard!"

I lunged forward, reminding myself at the last minute not to touch her. "Take the fucking knife and slice the inside of your fucking arm from the elbow down! Go on, do it properly, *Mother*! Do it! Go on, bloody kill yourself. Do it! *Do it*!"

Blood throbbed in my ears. I fancied I could taste it in my mouth like a vampire on a high from a recent kill.

Mother looked up at me from beneath those long eyelashes, her eyes filled with tears.

I didn't think even then that she had the guts to do it, but when the skin peeled back from either side of that knife as she drew it down her arm, as the blood spilled…as she cried out in pain…as she put her forehead down on the table…as the knife dropped from her hand…as her breaths became ragged, I knew, I knew then that she had never loved me. *Never*.

I walked out of that room and out of that house and ran back to the tree. There, I climbed to my branch and watched to make sure she never raised her head again. And I sobbed.

Chapter Fourteen

The winds of life blow in many ways; a harsh northerly gust, a soft southerly breeze. Times change, we move on. Phases pass in the wink of an eye. Where did my youth go? How did I become a man and not even notice? The wispy puff of the south wind enters life, calming the tornado.

***

Mother's funeral had come and gone. I think my father attended out of respect for the woman he once thought she was. I really don't know the real reason he chose to go, but I stayed away. I feared that it would upset me too much. I know that sounds odd, but the thought of looking down into that grave thinking that things could have been different might've made me feel sorrow for her. I did not want to reveal how hurt I was. Didn't want to cry.

I had graduated school and begun working. Since witnessing Mother's death, something within me stilled. The rage that was forever roiling in my guts, tainting my mind and making me a sullen, obnoxious child, had faded.

Father and I continued as before, living at the cabin, sometimes fishing together on the banks. Life felt calm, the surface of my internal ocean flat, soft mental peaks lapping quietly.

Until I met Janice.

She was a nurse. I first noticed her when I had been called to clean up a *spill*. A patient had been sick on the floor of the ward that Janice worked. It was my unfortunate duty to sanitise the floors. Sometimes I was asked to ferry patients to and from the operating theatres. Although the job didn't pay well, nor was it something I had really aspired to do, it was steady employment.

"Oh, here's the porter. Now don't you worry, Mrs Fallshore, it'll all be cleaned up and we'll say no more about it." She had her hand on the patient's brow, smoothing her hair back from her face.

I did get a shock. No one, apart from my father, had really looked at me. I mean *looked* at me as if I was special or needed, and it came as quite a surprise that this nurse should do so. I must have appeared a fool, leaning on my mop handle, face hot and sweaty, my Adam's apple bobbing up and down, chafing against my shirt collar.

I cleared my throat to ease some of the tension. Janice remarked later that she took it to be a sign that I was annoyed at having to clean up such a mess, that she was in the way of me completing my task.

Of course, I assured her that this simply wasn't the case. Admitting she had quite literally taken my breath away, something I never thought would happen to me. I had always imagined life being just me and Father living together with no room for anyone else.

The fact that Janice was soothing her patient as vomit dripped from the hem of her uniform furthered my admiration of her. She was a true trooper. I suppose you could say that I had fallen head over heels in love the moment I saw her. I was quite astounded by the roar of emotions that sallied forth within me, my head light as the proverbial feather.

Janice. What can I say about her? To me, she was absolutely beautiful. She had the aura of one who is continually kind, and everything she did, every movement, was graceful. Janice always had a smile for everyone she met, always listened to what others had to say. She was always happy, which made us an odd pair. I don't think I had ever come across a woman like her, nor would I in the future.

I saw her many times after that. It seemed that wherever I went, there she was. Maybe she had in fact been there all along, and I just hadn't noticed.

One day I sat enjoying a ham sandwich in the hospital canteen, while reading another book of poems that my father had given me at Christmas. Someone sat a tray full of food down on the table I was occupying, and, rather than look up, as I rarely courted company, I continued chewing and reading.

"You don't mind, do you, if I sit here?"

I recognised her voice right away, having replayed it in my mind since the first time I had heard it. Lifting my gaze from the page, I studied her tray before I answered. She too had a ham sandwich, but made with brown bread.

I recall straining my mind for something to say. Not to impress her (women had never entered my mind in the romantic way until I saw Janice) but to respond to her, to say *something*, anything at all.

"Uh, no, of course not." Inwardly, I groaned, my words hardly something an experienced man would have said.

"I have that book. Good, isn't it?"

I think that may have been what cemented it. That she shared my taste in poetry.

"Yes. My father bought it for me." I blindly gawped at the pages, not able to look at her just yet.

"My favourite is, 'How the wind blows'."

I wanted to look at her, to discuss that poem, to find out why it touched her as it did me. To tell her that the one I liked the best was entitled, "Dark Defence" but of course, I wasn't able to let her know just why I preferred that particular sonnet. I felt inadequately skilled in the verse of romance, an amateur in the game of love, to express at that time how I felt.

The silence stretched between us until I heard her sigh and start to unwrap her sandwiches, the clear wrap rustling slightly as she pulled it from the plate.

When she sighed, panic struck me. I didn't want her to feel uncomfortable and leave the table, finding someone more amenable to have lunch with. I remember taking a deep breath, trying to still the quakes within, and looked up at her.

"I like that one too," I said.

It sounded lame even to me, but she didn't flinch, nor look at me oddly. She just smiled, and for the first time in my life, something inside me melted.

I braved my tumultuous emotions and closed my book, placing it down on the Formica table next to my now empty tray.

"Oh. Are you leaving?"

Her voice sounded soft, wounded. I looked at her then, felt my face go hot, saw hers show signs of disappointment.

"Uh. I can stay, for another ten minutes anyway."

And so it went, we eased into conversation about the poems, and I found that I thoroughly revelled in her company, and she appeared to enjoy mine. Somehow, a date was set for meeting after work. For the life of me can't recall how that came about, such was my dreamlike state at that time.

We met at seven p.m. at The Blue Star.

Chapter Fifteen

At times, a new world presents itself to us mere mortals and it is up to us as to whether we see it. Vast lands stretch ahead, unexplored horizons, the Earth begging our feet to tread upon it. Were my boots thick soled enough to travel down this road?

***

I saw a new world when I entered The Blue Star, a modern haven for the young. Popular music emanated from hidden speakers, jovial voices and ribald laughter abounded. Even though alien, I felt welcome, my past firmly cemented. I became aware that I could begin again, start my life afresh.

Though never ashamed of what I had done, I yearned to be accepted by Janice, even at this early stage, not wanting any of my acts—that she would undoubtedly consider as horrendous—to come to her attention.

She was sitting to the left of the door upon a carver chair. Her handbag by her feet, ankles crossed, she looked so young, so fragile.

I mustered all the courage I had, and asked, "Would you like another drink?"

Her smile really did reach her eyes, the corners crinkling. I noticed the way her straight hair fell onto her shoulders. Brown, like deep, rich chocolate. And her eyes, they matched her hair.

"Orange juice, please. Early start for me in the morning," she said.

Her voice sounded overly bright, and in hindsight, I know that she had been attracted to me, even though I seemed a little strange. I made her uneasy, though she couldn't explain why. Of course, I put that down to my complete lack of courting skills and she readily accepted my explanation.

The bar was relatively clear of patrons, being served took no time at all, and before I knew it, I was back at her table, dumbly holding two orange juices. I was unsure of where to sit. In the carver beside her, or opposite? Opposite won.

Our conversation was somewhat stilted at first, having lost the ease that we'd gradually achieved at our lunchtime meeting. I recall fiddling with a beer mat, stripping the outer layer until no graphics remained, filling the unused ashtray with curly paper.

Until she asked what I thought of the poem "Dark Defence".

I didn't quite know how to answer. How do you tell someone, who you would like to get to know better that the words of a debauched poet touched you, rang certain bells within you, so that you felt someone out there actually understood you?

"I like the mournful prose," was all I could come up with.

"Don't you find yourself feeling sympathy even though the character has committed heinous crimes? That he is misunderstood in some way?"

Janice had mirrored my own feelings. Something I had hardly expected. I loved her even more then, and absurdly wanted her to hug me, to wrap me in her arms and make me feel special.

"Yes, most definitely," I agreed.

From that moment on, we filled our time discussing the poetry book again, and the evening sped by. By ten o'clock, it was evident we really should part company but neither of us wanted to do so. Rising from my seat, I remember saying, rather boldly for me, "Could we meet again? After work? Or for lunch in the canteen?"

I must have sounded desperate. The fact that she smiled *and* accepted my invitation blew me away. I was fast becoming attached to this girl.

***

Time moved swiftly while I was seeing Janice. You could say that I was in my "normal mode", living as others do, branching out into the adult world of finding a partner, securing your heart with another of like mind.

Father enjoyed Janice's company, embracing her into his life with gusto, clapping me on the back for meeting such a fine fish, as he put it.

Janice did comment on my gentlemanly demeanour, puzzled and somehow offended by the fact that I had not made any sexual moves upon her. It was due to my total lack of experience, my reticence. She thought that I did not fancy her enough and began to make comments regarding her looks, her figure.

Thus came the time when I told her a little about myself, that I was a virgin, unversed in love of any kind, except what my father had bestowed on me. I explained a little about my mother, how she had been in life, her sinful profession. I painted the picture as I saw it, Janice soaking up my verbal images, interpreting them as only she could, frown upon her face, compassion evident.

This eased the tension between us. She didn't press nor approach me sexually for quite some time, preferring to build up a trust between us. I found it hard to believe a woman could care for me, as my mother had not.

This suited me. Although I knew I was in love with her, and was able to engage in petting to a degree, I did know that I would need special stimulus in that department. Whenever I'd think of Janice in my room at night, I couldn't bring myself to climax without thinking of her dressed in the gymslip and knee-high socks that my mother had worn when she'd meet with certain customers. When the time came for Janice and me to have sex I would have to keep my thoughts of debase things firmly inside my head.

Luckily, society was lenient in my youth, so before our marriage, Janice was able to move into the cabin with myself and Father without it being frowned upon. We grew to love one another immensely and it was this love I believe enabled me to live as others did.

Our wedding day dawned drab and wet, a quick registry office ceremony witnessed by Father and a man he worked with, followed by drinks at our favourite haunt, The Blue Star.

Janice looked so young and beautiful that day, her simple ivory suit complementing her figure, the small spray of red roses a vibrant splash against it. Her cheeks were flushed and shiny, her eyes sparkling. I felt an overwhelming need to protect this woman, to keep our love safe, thus keeping the demons at bay.

Janice's parents, who were strict Catholics and aghast at our Pagan marriage, didn't attend our wedding. Janice rarely visited her family. Over the first two years of our union the family bond eroded. Janice appeared not to mind, seemed happy living with Father and me.

She said once, "All I need is you, John."

Her words will always stay with me, and it made me feel wonderful that this woman didn't need anyone but me. *Me.* My, how proud I felt. How big and strong and protective. At last I realised a female could love me.

Nighttime relations started on our wedding night, and I found that upon the actual consummation, it wasn't as difficult to perform as I had feared. Everything being so new kept my mind occupied on Janice alone, for a time.

When Janice announced her pregnancy, I felt quite nonplussed. I hadn't particularly thought about her conceiving, so wrapped up were we in each other. But, I did feel the paternal bond almost immediately as we planned how things would be, how we wanted them.

Everything considered bad lay dormant at that time. I did not think of debase things. I suppose it was because I was settled in my life. Finally I was loved, unconditionally, wholly.

Then two of us became three.

Edward was born in the place of our work with a lusty infant's yell at four twenty-two in the afternoon. Janice wasn't in labour long, just six hours, and I remember going to the telephone booth to ring Father.

"John, take care of him, son."

I felt an affinity with my father then, tangible even down the telephone line, and I wondered if this was how he felt when I had been born. The way he had cared for me as a child was second to none. I vowed to be the same father figure to Edward: trustworthy, caring, and loyal. And I would make damn sure Janice felt the same.

As it turned out, she adored Edward. The relief that she wasn't like my mother was immense, and I really did feel lucky to be living the life that I was. I should never have doubted that Janice would love our son. It was obvious she was nothing at all like my mother.

We moved from the cabin to a Council house in Hubert Lane, a two-bedroom abode that fitted our requirements nicely. Suburban life seemed to embrace me; the community spirit covered us like a cloak. We belonged.

Having a newborn in our home brought back memories from the past. I loved my son, doted on him, yet I had been able to kill another baby. If someone had taken Edward away, dropped him in the canal, I couldn't see myself being able to live, to carry on.

I had a confusing hour or two while cuddling Edward on the sofa one day, watching him while he slept, his tiny fingers unfurling. That I felt such love for this baby and none for the other one. That I would never harm this child, yet had no qualms about what I did to *that one*.

Tears stung my eyes. I grew angry with the overcrowding thoughts. Was this what guilt felt like? Was I starting to feel bad about the things I had done? There was no doubt that they had felt right at the time, but now, with my own baby in my arms, it felt as if killing that baby had been committed by someone else and not me.

And I knew Janice would think me heinous if she should ever learn the truth.

Unable to understand these feelings, I abruptly turned them off and concentrated on what I had now in my life. A wife whom I adored. A son who was my world.

I wanted to forget the past and be the person I now was. Not that horrible monster that was driven by his thoughts to do such terrible things.

And for a time, I did.

Chapter Sixteen

The sharp sting of the north wind strikes when you least expect it. We become complacent. The sea becomes choppy, waves ebb and flow. The demon is never completely banished however much you pretend it is.

***

I can see from reading over this account that my earlier years with Janice really did mellow me. My inner anger was almost obliterated and I do believe it would have disappeared completely had we stayed in the relative safety of the cabin.

Having lived in Hubert Lane for thirteen years (Edward had grown up into a fine young man), the return of my inner devil came as quite a shock, so long had I been without it.

The evening had started quite the same as any other. I had been stargazing, using my beloved binoculars, and the new telescope we had purchased that year, plotting the stars on my chart. Janice was in the kitchen doing the ironing. Edward stood on our street corner where I could see him, talking to his friends, some of them girls. I knew them all, having been there for several years.

I didn't pay them too much heed but could hear their chatter rise up through the open window, their laughter reminding me that their childhoods couldn't be farther removed from mine. It wasn't the fact that the blonde girl had offered Edward one of her cigarettes right in my line of vision. No, it wasn't that. It was what he told me later in the evening when he came in for the night.

"Lucy Berry's a right mean one."

Edward slouched down on the sofa, chin hidden in the lapels of the coat he still wore, shoulders hunched. I looked at Janice and she nodded, affirming that I should deal with "girl troubles".

"Why's that, son?"

Edward scowled. "I asked her if she'd be my girlfriend and she laughed at me, like I was stupid or something."

I clenched my teeth, my jaw muscles pumping. It was a typical girl response, so I had learned, yet it brought out such a rage in me, an ire I had thought was gone, extinct, that it knocked me off balance. I fought to hold the anger back as it seemed alien now, and unnecessary. The amount of anger didn't gel with what had caused it to erupt.

"Well," I began, not knowing what to say, "If she doesn't want to go out with you, that's her loss."

I recall hoping I had used the right figure of speech. Edward was popular. Having by-passed that section of my own life, I was anxious to ensure I got my responses as a father correct. Ridicule from my son would have cut deeply.

It appeared that I had indeed given the correct response as his face brightened and his head popped out from his jacket like a tortoise from its shell.

"Yeah, I could ask Kelly out instead!"

I frowned. Surely he didn't mean *her*?

"Kelly? Kelly Thomas?"

Kelly was the daughter of the Lane's resident scum. I kept my shock to myself knowing Edward would only pursue Kelly with more fervour, should Janice or I oppose it.

"Yeah, she's nice."

I disguised my sigh of irritation with a yawn. "You do that, son."

I smiled, and hoped it was convincing. The anger that had surfaced at my son's rejection seemed to float off again, which relieved me somewhat. Gone were the days of dark, violent thoughts and acts. Though they were the right things to do at the time, they had no place in the life I led now. I did not want them returning, messing up the stability I had built around myself.

But it was not to be. Inner demons can only be caged for so long before something or someone releases them. It was hearing Edward's teenage tears through the dividing bedroom wall that did it.

I lay in my bed listening to his tears, the sound of them ripping me apart inside. I didn't feel I should go in his room and comfort him, yet at the same time I wanted to let him know I was there for him. I felt at a loss. Then it came, the inner rage, encompassing me. I gave in, embraced it, and let it take me where it wanted.

The beast had returned.

***

I took to looking out of our bedroom window with vigour any chance I got. Scoping the lane for any signs of Lucy Berry and watching her through my binoculars. Hate festers from even the most subtle of slights, coiling round the heart and mind like a snake squeezing its prey.

While watching the Lane, I had also let my anger reach out to other, unsuspecting residents. It was amazing what one saw when watching, I mean *really* watching. Unaware, going about their daily business, I watched them all, but especially Lucy Berry.

My inner voice had returned with quite some force, smashing into my carefully erected barriers. So much so, that Janice had begun to ask if I was all right.

"Is anything bothering you, John?"

"I just feel a little out of sorts," was my standard response.

I had no idea how I could tell her how I was feeling. There was no way that she could possibly understand. Oh, I knew she adored our son just as I did, knew she would understand why I felt as I did towards Lucy Berry. Even she had felt anger towards the girl for hurting Edward. However, Janice's compassion overruled her ire and the incident was soon forgotten when it appeared that our son had forgotten it himself.

My devil did not allow me to forget and I changed back to the sour person I once was, relishing in terrible thoughts. Outwardly, I appeared relatively the same. But inside, a fire was burning and it wouldn't extinguish until I dealt with the arsonist who had lit it.

Chapter Seventeen

The essence of John Brookes was back—to stay.

***

The sickness had returned. As I write, I have changed from the mellow man I believed I had become back into the person I believe I was born to be. I was almost relieved to return to my old self again. My blasé self was once more a living, breathing entity in my soul. Ah, to live again!

***

Who did I pick that day? The woman with the bouncy curls in her hair and the spring in her step? The man wearing the grey pinstriped suit and black-rimmed spectacles? Or Lucy Berry, the bleached blonde floozy with the cigarette dangling from her lips?

Decisions, decisions. So many to choose from, yet for me, so few. Only those who had slighted Father, Janice, Edward or myself qualified for my particular brand of retribution. They had to have a certain thing about them that drew me.

Lucy's mother, or Bouncy woman as I thought of her, had a spring in her step all the time, and I wanted to stop that spring. I needed to give her something to be so un-springy about, bounding along as she did, smile plastered across her face even when she was alone. She thought I fancied her, which made me sick. A quick slash

71

across her face with a meat cleaver would wipe that grin away. Food for thought.

As for Pinstriped Man, he acted as though he was on a mission, walking along as if his backside were on fire. He took purposeful strides and had meaningful arm swings. Got control of his life, that one. I'd like to stop him, make him wake up and smell the coffee. Show him that he needed to relax, and teach him that life can be joyful. I'd give him something to think about. I'd heard that the man abused his wife, and this made me mad as well. Cutting his balls off with a pair of blunt scissors would do the trick.

No, out of the three subjects, Lucy Berry was one who needed to be taught a lesson. She stood around with her friends, striking poses, head cocked to the side, cigarette resting upon lips that were too young to taste it. And she flaunted herself, revelling in the testosterone emanating from the young lads she hung out with. Throwing her head back when she laughed, she basked in their adoration. She was just asking for it. I would only have to follow her. Matching her footsteps would be enough. Whispered threats would make her soil herself. Food for thought? No! This is your lucky day Lucy Berry. You've been chosen! You're my star.

She was the one.

I knew her routine. I had been watching my three targets on and off for the past month. I saw them in the Lane. Janice thought I had taken up stargazing as a serious hobby now. Bless her for believing me, for accepting what I said without question. She was such a dear soul.

I followed and watched Lucy through my binoculars as she usually stood on the corner, to the left of our house, sitting on the street sign, obscuring the name of the road for visitors. Around seven each evening, she set up residence with Kelly Thomas, followed by a group of lads who walked up for their usual gathering. She dealt out cigarettes like a pack of cards, her hot breath puffing into the air even before she lit up. One lad does not take a cigarette. Edward.

She stayed there for a couple of hours. They messed about, pulling each other's trousers down, or up into what I heard was called a wedgie. I was fascinated that they found this waste of two hours productive. I watched raptly at how they wasted their time, filling it with meaningless actions. Most of all, I just saw her. My eyes focused on her face, travelling down her body, and I felt my muscles tense, as I got annoyed at the way she portrayed herself. What must her mother be thinking, letting her go out in such a short skirt with a vest top on and her pubescent breasts on show? I shook my head.

A light drizzle had begun to fall that night. There they were, on the corner, as usual. I had to angle my binoculars towards the left to watch her. I got annoyed when she moved out of my view. I had to strain my neck against the wall to capture the scene, the plaster cold, giving me a crick in my neck later in the night. That was an added irritation, as if I needed anything else to spur my hatred of that girl. She soon moved back to her seat on the street sign, enabling me to have a more comfortable position.

She had taken a hooded top from her bag and put it on, carefully placing the hood over her head, so as not to mess up her perfectly straight hair. She looked better covered up.

I saw the light had faded, the street lamps giving off their foggy orange glow. I moved away from the window, reaching for my black bomber jacket with the balaclava in the right hand pocket, gloves in the left. I put my coat on, zipped it to the top, and left the bedroom, tripping lightly down the stairs with Bouncy Woman's spring in my step.

"Going to the pub for an hour, love!"

"No stars out tonight then?"

Janice always replied the same way. I looked at her, took in her pretty face, the way her eyes softened as she looked back at me.

"Yes. There are a few stars out tonight. I just fancy a beer, that's all. Going to call Edward in, on my way past, all right?"

"Oh, right ho. See you in a while then." Her face looked worried when she added, "Will you be long?"

"Not long, no."

I smiled at my wife, and she smiled back, uncertain of the change in me, unsure as to why I had taken to going to The Blue Star alone. Perhaps she suspected me of having an affair. Knowing Janice, she would be blaming herself, thinking I wanted to get away from her, that she had done something wrong. I wish I had spoken to her at this time, put her mind at rest, but I didn't. I took her for granted. I know that now.

Dismissing these thoughts, I left the house, approaching the corner of our Lane with the gang of kids adorning it.

"Hi, Mr Brookes!" they chorused.

"Hi there, kids! Edward, time to go in, son."

I walked past, jaunty of step, smile on my face, the darkness hidden within. I strode round the corner, across the main road, into one of the small alleys that made up our estate's walkways. There, I waited. She'd walk some of the lads home first, Kelly having gone in already, then come this way to go back home to the Lane.

I put the balaclava on to hide the smoke-like breaths that left my mouth; they dissipated into the wool, leaving a wet residue. I remember it made my lips sore, annoying me. I took my woollen gloves from my other pocket and put them on over fingers that were rough like a charwoman's.

I looked inside myself and examined how I felt. A little nervous, perhaps a bit guilty—it being the first time I had succumbed in years—and slightly excited. My heart was beating fast, seeming to rise up into my throat. My Adam's apple felt alive, quivering, but quite painful. My nose ran a little. I used my hand to stem the drip onto the facemask. Wool against wool made a squeaking noise, sounding highly audible in the quiet hidey-hole. Slowly and quietly, I rubbed my nose. I did not want any sharp movements. The bush I was concealing myself in would rustle and move.

I recall feeling elated, thinking, "She's coming! Oh here she is!" Walking across the main road, jaywalking I might add, with her hands in her pockets, hood up and her head down. She was very unwise, making herself such an easy target this way. No hands free to protect herself should she fall. No eyes looking forward to see the danger. Perfect. She had less of a swagger now. Less self-assurance. I would teach her.

She walked past, her trainers squelching along the wet pavement, laces free and slapping at her bare legs, leaving muddy slash marks across her shins. Another unwise move on her part. She could trip on those laces. No common sense at all, this one. I counted fifteen paces, and emerged from my hiding place and followed her. Lucy Berry had a way to go down the long alley with no houses on either side, just wooden fencing and trees that bordered expansive fields. The streetlights here were few and far between. One at each end and two spaced out down the middle. Dark and ideal for my plan.

Lucy's shoulders tensed. She heard my footsteps. I was deliberately heavy footed. She walked a little faster, and I immediately matched her stride. Her head snapped upright, and I imagined she had her eyes trained on the end of the alleyway towards her escape, and her ears tuned in to the movements behind her.

She upped her speed, slowly at first, as if she did not want me to notice the change of step, then faster. Her breath trailed behind her as she puffed with a little terror and the unexpected exertion. I hoped her heart was beating faster; that her stomach had turned to mush, and the sound of her blood was pounding round her head like the whoosh of a wave crashing upon the beach.

I matched her step again, and it was then that she decided to run. She had three quarters of the alley to travel; yet she ran. I sprinted up behind her, closing the gap with the speed of an ocelot. She turned slightly, but with the hood on, her straight hair whipped in a sheet across her face making it impossible to see me clearly. The girl let out a strangled gasp, followed by a sob. She knew a man was gaining on her, so this should have been enough to stop her from being so flirty, but my mind was not listening. I wanted to take it a step further.

I was as close as I could get, and I clasped my hand over her face, closing my palm over her mouth. She let out a muffled cry as my other hand grabbed her left upper arm. I steered her, struggling, into the small trees that ran parallel to the fence. Branches snagged my mask, but I was moving too quickly for them to tug my cover free. I felt her mouth moving under my hand. Oh, a feisty girl, trying to bite!

Keeping her facing away from me, and shoving her forwards up against the fence, I adopted what I hoped was a menacing tone. My voice came out flat, without emotion. Even I did not recognise myself.

"Do you want to live?" I asked.

She sobbed, nodding frantically, her eyes squeezed shut, tears slipping out from under her lids.

"Dirty girls like you deserve to be punished. Do you want me to punish you?"

She shook her head. I moved my hand down her left arm, and gripped her wrist, folding her arm back on itself, between us. For fun, I chose then to stick my thumb into the small of her back, while my fingers still held her wrist.

"I could stab you right now. No one would find you for days."

My breath came out in short sharp bursts, as did hers. For a moment, I was fascinated that our clouds of breath merged into the night sky, floating upwards until they were nothing. She broke down then, and finally I heard what I had been waiting for. The soft trickle of her urine, snaking down her legs, into her trainers. The steam coming from her lower limbs reminded me of when a dog takes a leak in the winter.

Pushing her harder into the fence, I jolted her upwards and back down again, enjoying the fact that the wooden surface would break her skin, maybe leave splinters and draw blood. Her face would show her ordeal and remind her of it for a while to come.

Muffled noises came from her mouth. Mucous dribbled from her nose had settled on my gloved finger. She tried to cry, but my palm restricted her being able to take a strong enough breath to enable the wracking sobs that longed to escape her lips.

"When I let you go, you dare not turn around. You stay where you are for five minutes. I will know if you move before then. If you do move and look at me, I will kill you."

My voice was so calm.

I let her go, and took a step backwards. With her legs bent slightly at the knees, her feet around twelve inches apart, toes pointing inwards, she leaned on the fence with her forehead for balance. Her arms hung loose and straight by her sides. Her hood half covered her face. Strands of hair, wet from sweat and tears and snot, stuck to her cheeks. Her eyes were still closed tightly. She muttered, "Oh God, oh God," several times, before saying, "Mum...I want my mum."

I backed out of the trees, walking in reverse, watching her, making sure she did not turn to look at me. She did not. Twisting round with speed, I ran, ripping off my mask while I did so, pulling off my gloves, running my fingers through my hair to tame the unruly mess the mask was sure to have made. Across the main road now, walking normally, upright, smiling. I really hoped she would learn, for her sake.

At the pub car park, I placed my mask and gloves as deep down as I could reach into the large Biffa bin that held all their waste. It would be collected by the morning.

Drinking my pint, I knew no one would suspect me. Thoughts ran through my mind. I replayed the events of the last twenty minutes or so.

When I returned home Janice asked, "Did you see anyone at the pub, John?"

I replied, "Yes, love. I had a pint or two with the landlord, but the bar was pretty empty."

She seemed relieved.

What was my final thought before forgetting the incident altogether and closing my eyes that night?

"That will teach you to hurt my Edward, you little tart."

I loved our son with a passion.

Chapter Eighteen

The voices are controlled. Separating oneself into two parts takes strength. Now that I have accepted that my demons are here to stay, I have embraced them once more, careful, ever careful to keep one side of me from the other. They must not spill over the line that keeps them apart.

***

The story of Lucy Berry being attacked spread through the Lane, as I knew it would. In jovial neighbour mode, I held my hand to my mouth, as did everyone else, when her mother, Bouncy Woman, related the tale to us.

"Poor girl, she was just walking the lads home, you know? Wasn't even that late at night! I'd keep Edward in if I were you. Who knows, this madman might like the boys too!"

Not so bouncy now, Lucy's mother crossed her arms under her ample bosom. Her cheeks, ruddy from indignation, inflated as she took in a breath and then let it out. Steadying her emotions, as her sigh came out ragged, she continued, totally ignoring Janice by my side.

"Anyway, John, how are you?"

She gave me what she probably felt was a saucy wink. My stomach revolted. After living in the Lane so long, I would have thought she knew I wouldn't stray, that Janice and Edward meant the

78

world to me. Still, I suspect she felt she could try, that even the most devoted of men could be swayed by her charms.

I recall thinking, *Not this man, lady. Try this game again and you'll see what you get.*

I had to still my inner rage, mask it so that Janice, and Bouncy Woman herself, didn't pick up on it.

"I'm fine, thank you. More to the point, how is Lucy?"

"Oh she'll be all right. She's a tough one, she is."

Janice took in a sharp breath, but Lucy's mother didn't appear to hear it. I knew Janice would be thinking Lucy might need some support at this time, not the brush-it-off attitude her mother had adopted. All Ms. Berry probably cared about was a few weeks worth of gossip chatting at doorsteps, and a good dose of much-craved attention. Janice wasn't of this ilk. She would have given Edward her full support had this kind of thing happened to him, and this knowledge only served to make me hate Lucy Berry's mother and love my Janice even more.

"What did the police say?" asked Janice. She was such a concerned person, always caring. I was glad she had asked that.

"Police? Oh, I didn't bother them with this! No fear! Not with them stereos I've got stashed in my spare room. Don't want them poking about, do I?" Bouncy Woman let out a harsh laugh, almost a bark, her breasts heaving along with her hilarity. "Anyway, all he did was scare her a bit. Made her piss her knickers and all."

"Oh!" Janice exclaimed, her sympathy for Lucy coming to the fore. She turned with tears in her eyes and stepped back into our house. For her, this discussion was closed.

I should have followed Janice inside to give her some comfort, but instead, I said, "Oh the poor girl." My face had adopted the look of a concerned neighbour.

"Oh John, you're so...nice!"

Again the wink, this time accompanied with a brush of her fingers along my forearm. Shuddering inwardly at her touch, I backed away to the safety of our threshold, as we had all been standing in our front garden discussing the tragedy.

"Well, a little niceness doesn't hurt, does it?"

"No John, it most certainly doesn't."

Her fulsome lips spread into a lascivious smile, showing yellow teeth.

"Well, I must be away now. Help Janice with the dishes. Sorry to hear about Lucy, I'm sure with a bit of special attention she'll be just fine."

How easy it was to slip into being the normal guy. Just as easy, too, to slide into my real self.

Bouncy Woman walked towards our gate. Her hand on the latch, she turned back looking at me in that leery way she had, and said, "Janice is a lucky woman, John. Wish I had met you first."

That wink.

I remember thinking to myself, *I'm glad we didn't meet back then*, before smiling, waving and going back indoors. Closing the door firmly behind me, I shut out that hateful woman and everything she represented.

Janice stood in the kitchen, her hands hidden by the bubbles in the sink.

"You know, John. Much as I don't like being spiteful, that woman really is low on my scale of one who has morals. Nothing seems to faze her, and I'm sure, and have been for a while now, that she has her eye on you. I had almost convinced myself, what with you going to the pub a lot recently, that you were seeing her!" She laughed the laugh of the worried, hiding how she really felt, keeping suspicion at bay.

I placed my arms around her waist from behind, nuzzling my chin into her neck. "Janice. Don't ever think there would be anyone in my lifetime that could come close to tempting me. I love you, and I love Edward. I love my father, and no one else. No one."

I must have sounded quite abrupt, as I felt her tense, her shoulders going rigid beneath my chin.

"You do believe me, don't you?" My tone was softer then. I had let part of myself bleed into the other. My hatred towards Ms. Berry spilled out in my voice when talking to my beloved wife. This made me hate the Berry woman even more.

Janice relaxed, her head falling back to rest against my cheek.

"Yes, John, I do."

Stilling the beast within me, I helped my wife with the washing up, drying the dishes, then making us a cup of tea to drink while we watched the television. A companionable silence ensued, while we waited for Edward to come in, then we locked up for the night and retired to bed.

Our lovemaking had new fervour that night, Janice clinging, grateful to have her suspicions quashed, myself trying to purge the hatred I felt for the Berry woman until the time was right to teach her a lesson.

Chapter Nineteen

Beelzebub ran through my veins. Once I had let him back into my mind, my life, I was a fool to think I could control him. He struck quicker, sharper than he had before. Not being able to quench my thirst with killing small animals, I suppose it was inevitable things would turn out this way.

***

The urge to teach Ms. Berry a lesson came upon me faster than I had anticipated. I felt it was some calling from God above, or the Devil below, harping at me to perform another task. I knew at some point she would have to be dealt with, I just did not know when.

Bouncy Woman. She of the bounding walk, hair so springy I had visions of it jumping from her head and bouncing off along the pavement. My mind envisioned a blonde curly wig upon a football, bounding merrily down our street, tresses lifting and falling with each spring. I imagined the football as Bouncy Woman's head, as it tried to cross the road, an oncoming car smashing into it, splitting the face apart, the brain flying in all directions, like pieces of sliced jellied eel. Quite an amusing thought.

I did, of course, have to watch her, to refresh myself with her habits. On occasion, I followed her to where she worked, to the places she frequented of an evening, just to get a feel for her. She was very irritating, and I almost had to stop myself from attacking her just for the way she presented herself.

Although she possessed big heaving breasts and a lardy rear end that shuddered with each step she took, she still thought herself attractive, and that others found her so too. I knew this, because she thought I fancied her. The idea of it made me come out in quite a sweat, as I found her revolting. How she could imagine that I would like her, when I am happily married to my beautiful wife, I could not imagine.

She bounced past our front garden fence this particular week and stopped, her hand atop one of my picket points, which annoyed me immensely, and stood, hip cocked.

"Hello, John!" she beamed.

I had been weeding, and so as not to appear rude, I said hello back as I always do to anyone who should pass the time of day with me.

"Seen anything you fancy, Mr Brookes?" she said, with her trademark wink.

Once again, the anger seeped into my bones, though she didn't know it. What a ridiculous question! I could not feel attracted to her, with her bright orange blouse partially buttoned up, showing a low cut white top underneath, her ample melons jumping out at me. Her short black skirt revealed pitted thighs, straining beneath her tights. Revolting blubbery lips, smothered in red lipstick that had collected itself in lumps in the corners of her mouth made me queasy. Even her teeth were stained with it. Her speech alone grated on my nerves.

"I beg your pardon, Ms. Berry?"

I tried to sound like I was amused. She must have thought as much, as she then chuckled and walked off swinging her ample backside, reminding me of a pregnant cow.

Recalling this incident and the re-telling of it to my wife, made me sure that Bouncy Woman was indeed destined to be my next star.

I could see her through my binoculars. Angled to the right this time, I had a clear view through the sides of her bay front windows. I had been watching her in her lounge, but now she had gone upstairs, I presumed, to have a shower. It was ten minutes before she went into her bedroom, turning on the light, leaving her curtains open. As it was dark, I had the totally foul view of her towelling herself down and applying talcum powder to her person. I wanted to glance away, not out of respect, but from repulsion. But to see this mission through until the end, I knew I had to keep watching. To feel such repugnance fuelled my hate, and justified my reasons for having to teach her a lesson.

Her thighs wobbled as she walked on her tiptoes to what I could only assume was a drawer. She stooped over, displaying her grotesque bottom. Seeing such a frightening thing made the world sway and my vision blur. I hoped she put clothes on soon. She must have been listening to music, as she flung herself around her room, tights in hand, swaying in time to a beat only she could hear. I thought to myself that I wished my binoculars could pick up sounds as well as sights. It would probably add to my annoyance, knowing what music she enjoyed.

I watched her get dressed, saw how she styled her hair, how she applied her make-up. She was going out. I would have to follow, of course. I was unhappy with her for upsetting Janice. It seemed to make it all the more reasonable in my mind to do what I did when it was for her, Edward or my father. I told myself that by Bouncy Woman approaching me in the manner she had last week, I could, in fact, be doing this for my wife.

I glanced to my left. Edward was on the corner, minus Lucy Berry. She had not been present with the group of teenagers since I had taught her a lesson. This, of course, made me happy that someone had taken heed of me.

The Berry woman came out of her house, approaching the group on the corner. I could hardly bear to watch her cannoning down the road. Oh, her bounciness really did get me to a point where I could almost thump the living daylights out of her, but I told myself to wait for the right time.

She stopped and spoke to the teens, hip cocked yet again. I could only imagine what she was saying. Edward looked shocked, his mouth had fallen into an "O" of surprise. I waited for her to leave them, and proceed down the alleyway, before going to the front door and calling Edward indoors.

"Yes, Dad?"

Edward stood in the living room doorway, his face showing concern. He was wondering if he had done something wrong.

I smiled at him to alleviate his fears. "What did the Berry woman just say?"

Edward reddened, moving uncomfortably from foot to foot.

"Oh, nothing much…"

"Edward, it's ok. You know I'm only being nosey! Come on, what did she say?"

"Oh, uh, that she betted us boys wouldn't mind having a woman like her for a girlfriend. We just laughed, you know. She was only joking."

After listening intently, I told Edward, "Ha! What a strange woman! Let's hope she was joking, eh? Else you'll have a worry on your hands! Go back out with your friends, son." I shook my head as if it were indeed the joke I had brushed it off to be.

"Ok, see you!"

Edward dashed back outside. White-hot anger roared through my body, enveloping me into such a frenzy that I knew this moment could not go to waste. Hurriedly I ran to our bedroom, collected the innocent looking carrier bag that I needed, slung on my coat, and headed down the stairs. The opportunity to see my dream through was upon me.

"Going out to The Blue Star. Got to dash! Call Edward in later for me!"

I did not hear Janice reply, as a roaring had filled my ears. Adrenaline coursed through my blood, making me feel quite giddy and sick. Controlling my emotions and posing as the good father, I waved to Edward and his friends, told them I was away to the pub for a spot of elbow exercise and I would see him later.

Chapter Twenty

Vengeance is mine. Ms. Berry would no longer attract anyone. Anyone at all.

***

I had to be sure she would go into town to the karaoke that was held in The Bar. She always walked through Southbourne — a series of fields and pathways with a small children's park in the centre, unlit by any street lighting, much to my advantage.

I warned myself to remain calm and not get out of breath. Mentally sorting out my mind, I had been scanning the path ahead through Southbourne. There she was, just coming up to the bridge over the stream. My carrier bag would rustle, I knew that, but if I was quick, by the time she heard it, it would be too late for her.

Pulling a new balaclava over my head, slipping on gloves and taking out my weapon covered in a sock, I hastily shoved the bag, containing clean dry shoes and trousers, into a bush for my return.

It was so dark, but the moon offered a dim light, and I was able to ascertain that it was indeed she.

With no time to think, I dashed stealthily up behind her.

The bank beside the bridge was sludgy, but I'd known I would get wet, so it didn't matter. I pushed her hard in the back, and watched her slip and slide the short way down into the stream. She let out a small "Oh!" of surprise, but the sound of splashing water muffled it. She unceremoniously sat slumped in the cold stream with her back to me.

A condensation had formed again inside my mask, making my lips and the skin surrounding them feel wet and slippery. Due to the forced swiftness of my mission, I couldn't control my breath as I had with Lucy. My heart thumped wildly, and it frightened me that someone might actually hear it.

I made my way down into the brook before Ms. Berry had a chance to turn around, carefully placing my weapon down on the bank. My feet made plopping sounds as I stepped down into the water, and I knelt down behind her. Placing my hand on those damn bouncy curls, I drew her head back slightly, and gripped her, so she could move neither left nor right. I checked to see that no one else was around. All seemed quiet, and thankfully, Ms. Berry herself had not uttered a single sound since I had startled her.

She moved her eyes to her right then, trying to see me, and they widened when she realised it was a masked man kneeling behind her. Reaching behind me, I patted the grass until I could feel my sock-encased weapon. Pulling the sock from it, I stuffed it into her mouth.

She panicked; her breath coming out in short, snotty blasts, quite like an angry bull. I watched her for a second, amazed that she had chosen not to strike me with her free hands.

It was then that I realised my mistake. I had left the small reel of fine wire in the carrier bag. I could not go back for it. My eyes narrowed in frustration, but quick as a flash, ever the entrepreneur; a thought came to my mind.

My voice, calm again, and so unlike my own, surprised me once more. "Get your tights off!"

She probably thought herself so alluring that the inevitable had happened, and someone was going to sexually attack her. Stupid, stupid woman. I would not lower myself.

Rocking from side to side, she was able to remove her tights. The slick squelching noise they made as she peeled them away from her legs sickened me. In the moonlight, her limbs looked like large blocks of cheese. I shuddered. She had such a high opinion of herself she probably thought I wanted to have sex with her because I thought she was God's gift to men.

She sat there like a suckling pig, mouth stuffed, and about to be trussed.

"Put your hands behind your back!"

My armpits dripped sweat, and despite the cold evening, I was relatively hot. Once she had complied, I snatched the tights from her hand and let go of her hair. Roughly shoving her head forward, I swiftly bound her hands together, making a figure of eight with the nylon before tying it tight.

"Lean back against the bank!"

Ms. God's Gift to Men would definitely think that she was about to be raped.

She did as she was told. I stood looking down at her, and she looked up at me standing just to her right. I wondered if she would recognise my clothes as her eyes looked like they were going to bulge out of their sockets and her snorting began again in earnest. Was she staring at me in this way through fear, or recognition? I could only pray that her fright was so paralysing she didn't recognize me.

I knelt down astride her. She was laying so far back against the bank, it would be impossible for her to escape as her legs were held fast by my position upon her.

I leaned forward for my weapon. It glinted in the light from the moon, a meat cleaver, thick and heavy, sharp and menacing.

She really did get on my nerves that night. Watching the snot shoot out from her nostrils was most disconcerting and very unbecoming of a lady. But then she wasn't a lady and never had been. Hadn't she proved that last week and this evening by her disgusting language to Edward? Telling him if he fancied what he saw…Dirty bitch.

No sympathy. None at all.

"Let out a sound, and I will kill you! Right?"

She nodded like the toy dog in the back of our car, head going in all directions.

I brought the meat cleaver up to her line of vision. She began gagging on the sock, making soundless retches. The wet mud had soiled her hair on the ends and sweat had begun to form on her brow and in the dimple of her chin.

Placing the cleaver in my right hand, I brought it to her right cheek with the blade pointing towards her ear. I pressed down a little to see if she would indeed make a noise, but she continued with her snotty emissions. I then jerked my hand and sliced her cheek clean off. It fell into the stream and lodged itself with the current against her pitted thigh. She fainted.

I noticed that for a split second after I had sliced, the wound on her face resembled brawn. Curious, I picked up the pouch of cheek from the water and examined it, then placed it in her hand.

Glancing from left to right again, not seeing anyone or anything untoward, I rinsed the cleaver in the water, before lopping off her other cheek. I did this quite calmly and easily. I am not even sure if she was breathing. I placed the second freshly cut cheek in her other hand.

Her face was a nasty mess. Blood had streamed from the wounds, down into her hair, and then made its way into the water. I read somewhere that if wounds bled, it meant the heart was still pumping, so this was quite a relief.

I could not have planned it better. I would leave her sitting there in a dead faint against the stream bank, water taking away any evidence of me. Bouncy Woman was far enough away from the water's edge that she wouldn't drown. A toad or two might've come along to feast upon her face, but it was what she deserved.

I climbed cautiously from the water, keeping low as I came level with the bridge on my right.

Seeing absolutely no one around, I got my bag. I removed my gloves and mask and began walking.

The Blue Star was five minutes away. Having frequented the place for years, I knew I could get in through a back door used by employees. This led to a short corridor, then to a public toilet. I entered; looked around to ensure I was alone, and slipped into a cubicle. Changing my sodden trousers, socks and shoes, I placed them in my bag.

Dry from the waist down, and drying my hands and face, I went to the bar to enquire if the billiards tournament was on that night. I knew it was not, but I wanted to be seen asking.

I left the pub, walking the main road home, avoiding Southbourne.

***

"Alright, love?"

Janice was so caring.

"Yes, I just need some things put through the washer."

Janice took the bag. Removing the clothes from it, she asked, "What on Earth have you been doing, John? These are soaked!"

I didn't know what to say, felt my mind clamming up on me as I hadn't expected Janice to ask that. She was usually so quiet and accepting.

"I uh, fell over the bank a couple days ago on the way back from work, landing in the edge of the stream at Southbourne." My laugh sounded hollow, and Janice frowned. "I felt so stupid."

"So why didn't you stick the clothes in the washer *then*?" Janice bent down to place the clothes in the machine and my heart hammered. I was lying to my wife and it didn't sit well. Yet I could hardly tell the poor woman what I *had* been doing. My mind raced.

"I'm sorry, love. I just forgot. Remembered the bag when I spotted it by the front door on my way in just now."

"By the front door? John, are you messing with me, because that bag wasn't there earlier." With stiff movements, I put the detergent into the machine drawer, knowing I was on dangerous ground with my wife.

"It was by the door outside, sitting in the bush." My face flamed.

She didn't question me further, just looked at me oddly, nodded and said, "Edward was telling me what Ms. Berry said to him outside earlier. With what she said to you last week, I think she's got a cheek, she has!"

I nearly choked.

I changed, made sure my clothes and shoes all went through the machine and were dried before we retired for the night. I cut up my gloves and mask, and made a tiny bonfire in a metal bucket in the garden. I did not quite know what to do with the cleaver.

Janice watched from the kitchen window. She didn't say a word.

Chapter Twenty-One

Reflection: a time to piece it all together, to make sense of the past, and clear up any questions once and for all, before moving on to the future.

***

I feel quite exalted having just read my account from the beginning up to now. I had originally put pen to paper to try to understand myself, to know me, or rather people like me. Having digested everything I have written, I can put a name to myself now.

Deranged. Psychopath. Murderer.

What I have read about these conditions leads me to believe I am a classic case for a mental institution at best, a prison at worst. Yet I do not feel the slightest bit insane. Madness, not beauty, is in the eye of the beholder.

I can accept that as a child I felt unloved by my mother, that she became the target of my rages. When I could not hurt her, I hurt defenceless beings instead. She was the real target of my ire, but in my younger years, I was hardly able to inflict damage upon her. I could have kicked, pummelled and bitten her, but young as I was, I knew the repercussions of those actions wouldn't have been worth it. So it festered, turned sour, and moulded until she finally got her comeuppance.

My adoration of my father was nothing unusual, except maybe for the lengths I would go to in order to right the wrongs done against him. My baby half-brother being the first real victim of my murderous rages.

The baby was the symbol that my parents' marriage was truly over, that the things my father had done for Mother just hadn't been enough. Never satisfied, she had to go for that little bit of extra spice in her life, ending up with a belly full of her sins. I did ponder whether Mother actually knew who that boy's father was, and whether the man himself knew he had become a dad. I doubt that very much.

Thinking of Mother, the highlight of my life had been watching her die as the blood oozed from her arms. It is something I will never forget, nor would I want to. I am not able to turn certain scenes away, however hard I try. That lost little boy I once was wanders through my mind. Most times I see him struggling to make sense of what he is, what he might become. I see him reaching out to his mother with his arms only to be rebuffed, shoved away. I see him stroking his mother's hair when she is asleep from drinking the gin, moments in time that I pretend never happened, that I didn't touch her, hated her always.

Sometimes that child irked his mother to get a reaction from her. Other times he walked away defeated, knowing in his heart he wouldn't be loved by the one person he craved it from. I see him now, with chubby legs, toddling up to his mother, grabbing her skirt to steady himself, but she turns round and hauls him up by the arm, dangling him in the air, her other hand swift and sharp upon his bare legs.

Confusion, confusion on his face. Please love me, Mummy. No, I don't like these thoughts, but they are always with me, battling for supremacy against the darker, more sinister images.

When Janice came along, I could see how my mind went back in time, my writing almost totally different from the previous pages. My sane time. My normal time. Maybe my left frontal lobe began working properly in those years. Maybe the fact that my mother could no longer hurt us caused my brain to function normally.

I can't say I didn't enjoy those years, because I did. They were exciting in a different way. New things to discover, novel emotions coursing through me at the speed of light. Finding that I could love a woman *and* my own child with such a passion. A passion that I didn't realise existed for anyone other than my father.

After frightening Lucy Berry and hurting her mother, I visited my father. Maybe I needed reassurance? Perhaps I just felt the need to see him again should I get caught for my "crimes". I didn't see enough of him really, but he said he understood.

"You've got your own life to lead, John. No need to keep worrying about me. I've got my job, my fishing, and the cabin. I'm fine. Besides, I know where you are should I need you."

His wan smile made me feel fragile. His eyes looked a little rheumy, the skin on his face sallow. He was aging and I had barely noticed. Guilt spun me sideways so that I almost fell onto his sofa. Steadying myself I sat down, leaning my head against the backrest.

I remembered the day that bastard child was drowned and Mrs Drayton was at the cabin, sucking noisily on those mints. I thought of the look on my father's face that day. Remembered the care he had given me throughout my life.

I broke down, crying like I never had as a child.

"John! Son! Whatever's wrong, lad?"

Sniffling, I said, "Nothing, Dad. I'm just being daft that's all."

"Daft? It's not often I see a man cry, and if you of all people are shedding tears, there's got to be some substance to it, surely?"

I didn't want to worry him by telling him what I had done. I couldn't let him down. He wouldn't have understood why I had done those things.

"Just tired, Dad."

He sighed. "Can you afford a holiday?"

I sighed. "No. Not at the moment."

"Then I'll foot the bill, son. It'll do you good to get some clean air and clear the old head, eh?"

I didn't want to take the money, nor did I want to refuse it. I knew it would make him happy, knowing it had been because of him that his son, grandson and daughter-in-law had gone for a break and come back refreshed, feeling ready to take on the world again.

"Sure, Dad. Thanks. That'd be lovely."

It was then the next phase of my life began.

Chapter Twenty-Two

New climes and new sights refresh the mind. They do not, however, stop inner devils in their quest. I used to believe it was God who directed me but have since accepted the fact that some people are ruled by the Devil himself. And enjoy it.

***

We went to Chivenor, Devon.

The sea air and change of scenery worked wonders for clearing my mind. I felt refreshed, a new vigour encompassing me. Janice relaxed, her smiles more abundant. Edward loved it.

The surrounding towns were a joy to visit, and there were so many places to explore that were close to the caravan park in which we stayed. Just strolling round the campus made us all feel better, and the stress of our home life faded.

I had things on my mind, of course I did. Prior to that holiday, having committed my last crime had me thinking that if my inner devils were to prevail, I would have to be more careful. I couldn't kill so close to home any more, so it was necessary to broaden my horizons to escape detection.

Father had given us spending money so we could enjoy our holiday a little bit more. I shall always be grateful to the dearest man on earth. We were able to dine out instead of cooking in the caravan, pretend that we were well off. It's surprising how quickly you can grow accustomed to that way of life.

If Janice hadn't have had that headache, I don't think I would have done what I did next.

Curtains closed against the light, Janice lay on the bed, hand over her eyes. "It's a migraine, John," she said. "I'll stay in the caravan tonight; you and Edward go to the clubhouse. I'll be fine."

"Are you sure? I don't want to leave you if you're feeling poorly."

"I'm sure. I need the quiet."

I looked at my wife as she turned away from me, her eyes squeezed shut. I wondered what was going through her mind. The wet clothes incident came back to me and I felt a slight panic that maybe Janice suspected me of something. No, surely not?

I closed the half-sized door to our little room, and Edward and I made our way to the clubhouse. I put worrisome thoughts of Janice out of my mind. I felt claustrophobic, and if I didn't clear my mind soon...

A fancy dress competition was well underway when we arrived. Men dressed as women, women dressed as men, children a riot of butterflies complete with wings, and many a Spiderman flitted around on the dance floor.

We sat at a table near the front. The day before, Edward had made friends with a lad of his own age, who came bounding over.

"Want to go and play in the arcade, Ed?"

Edward looked at me. "Go ahead, son. Be back here by eleven and we'll head back to the caravan."

I slipped him twenty pounds, and he raced off with the vigour that only the young possess.

As I sipped my pint of beer, I watched the other holidaymakers. And then, I saw her.

My heart quickened, and, as sight sometimes plays tricks on us, I momentarily thought it was my mother, gliding across the dance floor towards me.

Her gait, style, was a carbon copy. Her features, not so much, but enough to startle me into thinking she had somehow come back, or that her suicide was all in my mind, her funeral some macabre trick someone had played upon me.

Could she actually be playing tricks on me from Hell? Before I knew it, I was out of my seat following the woman out of the clubhouse.

She looked distressed, swiping at her cheeks with the cuff of her black cardigan, her sniffles loud in the still air. Darkness had come to visit while Edward and I had been inside, a chill pervading the air. I remember thinking a frost may pepper the grass by morning, that this late September day would close and another one would open with autumn in full swing.

The woman made her way to the farthest of the caravans and down the meandering pathway that led to the "D" part of the site. I recall thinking, D for Devil, D for Death as I pursued her, stifling a chuckle at how quickly I had allowed my demons to overtake me when in the caravan I had felt lost and afraid. One minute, ensconced in holiday harmony, the next, chilled with hate and the desire to harm.

The woman veered towards a clump of trees that bordered the park. A park of caravans sat within a glade, fitting perfectly into what I had in mind.

The poor woman resembled another, so my mind was twisted by the need to upset her in some way. Thoughts tormented me, Mother's voice jeering my incompetence, my uselessness to such a degree that I felt myself careening out of control. This woman had a family somewhere, and somewhere there was a person who loved her. Regardless of my thoughts, I was prepared to snuff her out.

How would I feel if someone wanted to hurt Janice?

The thoughts were pounding through my head. The urge to hurt this woman was stronger than my need to walk away. It was wrong, but it didn't feel wrong to *me*. The force within overpowered my weakness while another little voice begged that no blood be shed. It would be difficult to hide such mess, and I had no covering for my face. Blood surged within me, bubbling throughout my body, roaring in my ears until I could hardly walk straight.

Staggering up behind her, following in her wake as she stepped into the woods, I tried to tread carefully, as the bark pieces on the ground shuffled with each step. I didn't want to alert her until we were deeper into the woods.

I heard traffic along the outskirts of the caravan park. As the darkness within me took over, and the darkness surrounding me enveloped us within its infinite chasm, I lunged.

Chapter Twenty-Three

During my assault on her, I was in turmoil. It was the first time I didn't feel fully in control. Maybe it was the different surroundings, the idea that I didn't know my way around enough to get away unseen. Whatever the case, it sated my demons a little. That it caused me to be unsettled was a price I just had to pay.

***

Lunging forward, I used my right hand to yank her head back by her hair and my left to cover her mouth. Peering round her head, I saw her eyes bulging in fear. She made snuffly noises like a newborn baby with a cold, and her arms flailed around like windmill sails.

I was quite strong in those days, so was able to step backwards, taking my hand from her mouth, but still gripping her hair, and force her to fall to the ground by kicking at the backs of her knees. Down she went like the proverbial sack of shit. She was a little winded, so taking advantage of it, I jauntily dragged her along by her hair a little further into the woods before her brain realized that she needed to scream.

The trees enclosed us from view, and she sobbed as she tried to pull my hands out of her hair. Doesn't it hurt when your hair is pulled as hard as that? The last time Mother had wrenched mine like that, I found I had a sore head the next day.

I knelt down behind her, replacing my left hand over her mouth, blood continuing to pound in my ears, excitement of the moment making me giddy.

She whimpered. The woman wasn't daft. She knew it was her turn. Her turn to be one of those women you read about in the papers over your bacon and eggs. Your tea with two sugars.

The most disturbing part of it was the fact that she had snot coming out of her nose and it touched my hand. It wasn't nice. That really irked me. I remember clenching my teeth until my molar with the filling gave me a sharp pain. I didn't feel excited anymore, just angry that her bodily fluid had defiled me. Like it was part of Mother tainting me.

I needed to adopt my scary voice. The one I used on Lucy Berry. The roller coaster emotions I felt at that time made me feel quite sick. Laughter, excitement, anger, all at once, churning in my mind and gut. I'm surprised I wasn't sick.

"Shut the fuck up!" My voice emerged as a growl.

She went silent, and her eyes grew larger, rounder, which seemed impossible since they were already bugging out. This pleased me, but I had to take my hand away from her mouth as the snot on my index finger needed wiping. It made me feel quite ill.

"Is that you?" she said.

What the hell was she talking about? Maybe she thought I was the one who had brought her to tears, the one who had caused her to walk out of the clubhouse and down this dangerous route. It really didn't matter because I did not care.

I positioned myself behind her with her head resting upon my knees. She couldn't see me as it was quite dark, the moon obscured by the canopy of leaves.

I looked at her upside down face, as she looked up at mine. She remained silent.

With my free hand, I got out my penknife and flicked it open with relief, knowing that this would be over soon, that I could go back as if nothing untoward had happened, meet Edward, and then return to the caravan to see if Janice was alright.

I smiled tightly, and if I were poetic, I would say my teeth, had they been on show, would have glinted, and my sneer would have been frightening. At one time, I used to try out my facial expressions in the mirror and scared myself on the odd occasion.

I let her see the knife and stroked her bare neck with it, sending her my message. Her eyes told me she knew it was over now, and that she somehow knew why I was doing this. She knew I picked her at random, that she was just unlucky. The woman began to struggle, flailing on the ground, arms and legs thrashing. I held onto her hair, my fist clenched tightly in it. There was a pause in her movements, and I seized my opportunity.

Her ivory neck gaped open all too quickly, like a pair of lips in a jolly smile. The wound filled with her blood and it gushed and oozed out in a satisfactory manner, none of it soiling my clothing or me. I shuffled backward as the liquid of her life began to trickle down the sides of her neck. I didn't want my trousers ruined.

Tossing her forward, she slumped onto the ground. I breathed in and out with short, sharp bursts, and I recall leaning against a large tree to gather my thoughts, to get myself into some sort of order.

Arcing my foot over the ground to level out any indentions or footprints, I wiped my knife on the ground and casually made my way out of the woods, relieved, and indeed very lucky, that my emergence wasn't seen by a single soul.

Chapter Twenty-Four

Panic is not something I usually feel. Normally, I am in control.
Still, there is always a first time for everything.

***

Going back into that clubhouse, I knew I had to look and act *normal*. That when the alarm was raised, when the woman was discovered, everyone would be racking his or her brains to remember anything just a little bit "off" that evening. I could visualize the police questioning patrons as I made my way back to my seat, which still, amazingly enough, had my half-finished beer on the table.

The sheen of sweat that I felt on my face made me feel paranoid, something I hadn't felt before, as if I had a spotlight upon me and everyone could see it. Smiling, I said to those seated nearest my table, "Have you seen Edward, my son? I've been looking for him, and got in quite a panic!"

I believed that would sufficiently dispel any later questions.

"Yes, love." A rather blowsy looking woman, flouncy frills on her blouse making me think of Shakespearian times supplied, "He came back about ten minutes ago, looking for you." Her cerise pink lips wobbled as she spoke, and after taking a huge gulp from what looked like a gin and tonic, continued, "Said to tell you he's gone to the bowling alley."

"Oh, thank goodness!" With a slightly exaggerated hand gesture, mopping my brow with my cuff, I sat, and downed the dregs of my pint. "Best be getting another drink then, now that I know he's safe!"

I walked off laughing, sure that I had acted normal. At that time, I was unsure of the worried feelings churning within me, and wondered why such misgivings were present this time around. I was used to feeling in control, of knowing that what I did was right. Perhaps it was the fact that I killed a random holidaymaker just because she looked like my mother.

Savouring the coldness of my lager, I made my way back to my seat, laughing at those in fancy dress, a crocodile line of freaks donned in their outrageous outfits. I applauded the winner, a rather obese woman dressed as Hitler (did she bring that outfit knowing she would enter? Complete with moustache?), and chatted as much as possible with my blowsy companion and her decidedly hangdog husband.

I felt better within myself, calmer, especially when Edward popped back for more funds.

"I won two pocketfuls of money from the two penny slots!" he said, a broad smile upon his face, cheeks slightly pink from excitement. "But then lost it all again when I played some more!"

"Never mind, son. So long as you're enjoying yourself. Be back here by eleven, ok? We'll have to be getting back to check on your mum."

"Yep. Cool!"

And he was gone, bounding off with his holiday pal. I felt a moment's happiness that my son hadn't had to endure the upbringing I had, that inner demons didn't visit him. No, I was sure he was safe from that torment.

Ten o' clock came round, overall a pleasant evening, save for my tumultuous stomach. It would be fine. I was sure of it. An hour to go, and many people had seen me sitting here, enjoying an evening of albeit strange entertainment. A band had started to belt out sixties music once the competition was over and the host for the evening had closed his strident voice, for which I was grateful.

"Where d'ya come from, then?" shouted Blowsy over the din of "Wild Thing" by The Troggs, poking my shoulder with a rather hard index finger.

I didn't want to give out too much information, didn't want to get too friendly with these people. The woman, the obvious force in the relationship. The man seemed there just for the sake of it, happy it seemed, to bumble along with her as his life-long companion. They really weren't my type.

"Oh, up north a bit." Smiling, I sipped my drink, glancing away from her to watch the dancers, hoping she would take the hint that I wasn't going to be very forthcoming.

"We *all* come from up north somewhere, what with bein' down in *Devon*, mate. You can't get further sarf than this, now can ya?"

My stomach roiled. Jaw clenching so that I was sure she could see my facial muscles working as I tried to stem my irritation, I offered a small laugh, hoping to appease her.

"I suppose we do, yes!" I felt claustrophobic, wanting to run away from this room and everyone in it.

"Us, well, we come from London, you know, *The Big Smoke*. Have a right old fuckin' laugh there we do. Got a market stall, sells cleanin' stuff, ya know, brings the money in all right! What d'you do then?"

My lips tightened. Agitation rippled through me, not liking to divulge anything about myself to what amounted to complete strangers.

"I work in a hospital."

"Ooooh you look like the doctor type. I was saying to my George here, he looks like the type that's a doctor. You can tell, you see, from the way you holds yourself. Upright and all that." She turned her jowly face to George, nudging the poor man in the ribs when he appeared not to have heard her, eyes glazed over, his only movement his arm moving up and down to bring his glass to his lips.

"I was saying, weren't I George, that I thought this bloke here was a doctor. I was right! What did I tell you, eh?"

This seemed to give her much pleasure, being right, and George smiled at me, tilting his glass slightly before returning his gaze to the dancers doing the mashed potato.

"Useless, him. No point tryin' to start a convo with that geezer. I tell you, I might as well be livin' with a bleeding statue. I does all the work on the markets, but *him*, he just sits at home. Reckons he's disabled, bad leg. My arse! I reckon he's just a lazy bastard meself."

She really was uncouth and reminded me of Lucy Berry's mother. I felt the surge begin, and knew I couldn't possibly let *it* happen again. Not twice in one place. Struggling with my emotions, I decided she really didn't need any answers, as long as I kept smiling and nodding, she was quite happy to keep spouting words at me.

I tuned into her again as she began relating some incident from her days at her market stall.

"Well, I says to her, 'If you dare fucking look at me like that again missus, you'll have my fist to deal with!' Well, that soon shut her trap, didn't it? There was no way I was going to replace or refund on a used fucking mop! Filthy dirty it was. She reckoned it didn't do its job properly. I said, 'If you weren't so bleeding dirty, mate, the mop would've cleaned up good and proper.' Disgusting she was. Looked like *she* needed a dip in the bloody mop bucket and all."

Some people annoy me to the degree that I could take whatever I had in my hand at the time and smash their faces with it. That night it was a pint glass, which I gripped so hard my knuckles bleached white. I wanted to maim this stupid, loud woman. Anything to shut her up.

Instead I kept smiling, laughed some, and waited for the next onslaught.

"Anyway, she trots off, dirty mop in hand, and I says to meself, 'I bet she hasn't cleaned her floor in a month of Sundays judging by the state of it.' Black as the ace of spades it was!"

Her raucous laughter split the air. Even over the noise of the band, many heard her, and still George sat there, an elbow-bending zombie. Inebriated as she was by too many gin and tonics, I realised that she would just keep on and on if I continued to give her an audience, so was much relieved when Edward came back out of breath from excitement, having won four pounds on a fruit machine that at his age, he shouldn't have even been playing. I didn't care. I had to get out of that ballroom!

I rose from my seat and stretched my muscles only to be faced with Blowsy doing the same.

"Here. I noticed you're in the van a few up from ours. We'll walk back with you, won't we George?"

George shrugged on his coat, mute.

Having walked from the clubhouse back to our caravan, with Blowsy hanging onto my arm for support, her stiletto heels clacking loudly against the pathway, her bawdy laugh renting the still air, I was relieved to climb into bed beside Janice to re-assess my evening prior to my fellow, albeit obnoxious, holidaymaker.

Chapter Twenty-Five

Surprisingly, the interview with the police was quite brief. A quick visit to our caravan, and they were away, seemingly satisfied with my account of the previous evening.

***

Relief streamed from my pores, sweat breaking out in what felt like torrents, small rivers rolling down my back, pooling in my trouser waistband.

"What on earth was that all about with the police, John?"

Janice, tousled-headed, migraine gone, sat sipping her tea.

"No idea, love. You heard as much as I did. Some woman was murdered here last night. It's really upsetting, isn't it, when you can't even go away on holiday without a crime being committed right under your nose!" I shook my head and sat beside her, sipping my own tea.

"Should we go home, John? If there's a murderer…"

"No, don't be silly. It'll be a one off. Can't really see a serial killer rampaging through the same holiday camp twice, can you?" I said.

"No. I suppose you're right."

She looked down at the cheap Formica table, scratched at its surface with a fingernail, looking perturbed.

"Feeling better today, love? Headache gone?"

She didn't look up at me, just frowned as if her mind was elsewhere, and then said, "Yes, thank goodness. I was in tears at one point after you left last night."

I did love her. She was so fragile looking. I didn't ask her why she had been crying, told myself it was because of the migraine. I didn't want to admit that maybe she was suspecting me of something, that my beloved wife had begun to doubt me. That it was I who had made her face look so strained, I who had made her appear more aged, caused the worry lines around her eyes. In hopes of seeing the spark in her eyes again, I blundered on with, "Fancy going into Barnstaple, do a bit of shopping?"

She brightened considerably. "Can we afford it?"

"For this week we can."

I felt sticky, the need for a shower immense. Finishing my tea with a burning gulp, I patted Janice's hand before rising, making my way into the tiny bedroom where I got the penknife from out of my jeans pocket and took it into the bathroom with me. Hanging my towel on the hook on the back of the door, I ran the water, testing the heat before stepping into the small cubicle. I carefully washed the knife, placed it on the floor outside the cubicle.

Letting the stream of water rinse away the policemen's visit, I thought about the murder. The worry. Unbidden, my erection bumped against the shower wall. Soaping up I began an urgent, if somewhat aggressive stroking of it, grasping myself in my hand, lost in the images my mind presented. Everything culminated into an almighty explosion, pent up emotions released.

Panting, I leant my palms on my knees, bending over to catch my breath, water pummelling my back. It would be ok. I was sure of it.

***

The three of us reached Barnstaple by mid-morning, the traffic jam into the town impeding our progress. Parking was another headache, but eventually we were strolling through the town with the usual seaside shops mixed with the familiar ones from home.

Why I suspected this place was any different from the usual shopping centre, I don't know. I suppose one thinks a holiday destination would be unlike home, that life for the town residents by the coast exists without a supermarket or the general stores the English need to survive.

We lunched at Banbury's. Janice was horrified by the prices.

"We could feed all three of us at home with a four course meal, for the cost of this lunch!"

I put my hand on hers, wanting to reassure her.

"It's ok. We have enough. This week is worry free."

Still, the uncertainty on her face was evident. The guilt as she took her first bite made me wish we had bought bread and fillings and packed our own lunch. She didn't enjoy the expensive sandwich one bit.

Edward, as kids are want to do, regardless of cost, polished off his prawn sandwich and tucked into a slice of cheesecake that would undoubtedly cost the same price as a whole one in Tescos at home.

I however, enjoyed it. For years, we had struggled without much money. I could have easily grown accustomed to the high life.

After a pot of tea, we resumed our trek of the shops, the undercover market our last port of call. Among the hand-knitted cardigans, the Women's Institute cake stall, and the second hand bric-a-brac, I found a gem of a gift for my father.

A small fishing hook set in its own carry case. The memory of the bass caressed me as I opened the case, feeling the sharpness of the hooks.

"Yours for a tenner, fella!"

I looked up at the stallholder, his hand already on a carrier bag, so sure was he of a sale. Part of me wanted to cut off my nose to spite my face, leave the silly man standing there dumbstruck as I walked away, cursing himself for being so forward. But the urge to please my father prevailed, to thank him for the generosity of this holiday was more important than getting one over on some Devon trader.

Handing over the money, I glared at his jolly face, felt a moment's sorrow touch me. He could after all be someone's dad, brother, son. My irrational urges to upset anyone who even slightly irked me gave me that uneasy feeling again. I wanted to be in control, and at that moment, I knew with certainty that I had already lost control.

Strolling from the stall to catch up with Janice at the cakes, I gave her shoulder a quick squeeze, wanting to let her know in some way how much she meant to me.

I recall thinking back then that I had ruthlessly killed and had gone about my business with abandon, yet I could still love others just like anyone else did. Perhaps I was normal, except I acted out my perversions instead of keeping them to myself. Maybe everyone felt as I did, only they didn't tell a soul. Surely, I wasn't the only person who visualised slicing someone's face off for things he or she thought offensive. I couldn't be the only man in the world who wanted to knife-stripe a man's back, his shirt flapping open to show the deep gouge my knife had wrought, just for giving my wife a look one second too long.

No. I'm not alone. We were all of the same mind. It's just that I showed my thoughts more often than not.

Chapter Twenty-Six

Sometimes an evening doesn't end as you thought it would.

***

After dining at the caravan park's restaurant—fish and chips for me, sausage and chips for Edward, Janice had a chilli—we went on to the clubhouse for the evening's entertainment.

Unfortunately, Blowsy and George, the former having no qualms about loudly discussing the previous night's murder, joined us.

Having introduced her and George to Janice, and finding out Blowsy's real name was Regina, we sat and suffered her rather colourful vocabulary for the next couple of hours.

"I was tellin' George that we go on bleeding holiday to get away from killing and crime, only to have some poor cow bumped off, throat slit, right on your bloody doorstep!"

Janice, to begin with, found Blowsy's choice of words startling, I could tell by the rise and fall of her eyebrows, but Janice relaxed as the evening wore on, so I knew she had dismissed the woman as a loud mouth with a kind heart. They chatted animatedly, discussing everything from the murder to the merits of dishcloths versus the scouring sponge.

I, however, struggled to find anything to discuss with George. He seemed quite content to stare into space, taking occasional sips from his pint glass.

This lack of interaction did give me time to think, to sort out the revelations of our holiday. I wondered what we could do the next day. If it was warm enough, I would suggest a day near the sea, perhaps Westward-Ho, although the tiny, sleepy place only housed a couple of shops and an amusement arcade that would hopefully keep Edward amused for the time we spent there. While we spent our minutes in strange company, I wondered about him in the clubhouse arcade.

"Fuck me! I tell you, your missus is quite a card!" yelled Blowsy, slapping my shoulder with her chubby hand. "Havin' a right old laugh, we are!"

"Good to hear that!"

Her jelly jowls wobbled in her mirth, bosom heaving as she took in a deep breath to steady herself. The gin had been replenished in her glass more times that I dared to count. Already three sheets to the wind, Blowsy showed no sign of actually shutting up.

Janice, however, looked like she had lost a pound and found a tenner, her features animated, eyes alive and dancing. I remember thinking, *let her enjoy herself. We'll be going back home before we know it. May as well let her hair down for once.*

"John," she said, her touch on my forearm reminding me how much I loved her. "I'm so glad we took this holiday."

I smiled at my wife then, took in her happiness, and said, "Me too!"

"Me an' all!" piped up Blowsy. "Normally, when we goes away, no bastard'll come and sit with us 'cos of old dopey bollocks here!" She gestured at George, almost smacking the poor, downtrodden man on the end of his nose as she waved her hand in the air.

"Oh, I'm sure it isn't George's fault!" protested Janice, ever the peacemaker.

"It bleeding well is, ain't it, George?"

"Hmmm?" he finally responded.

"You!" Blowsy continued. "The way you sit with a face like a smacked arse. Don't exactly encourage friendships, does it?"

"Suppose not," said George as he got up, keeping his gaze on a group of small girls playing grown-up dancing.

"Mine's a G and T if you're buying, George!"

Blowsy laughed, smacking the poor fellow on his rear as he made his way past her, unsteady from his limping leg.

"Yes, dear."

I thought then that he was a very resigned man. He looked like he just existed. And I had thought *our* life was uneventful and boring.

"Fuckin' hell! He's a bleeding nutcase, I reckon. Needs his head seeing to. Sits at home, he does, at the window all day. George don't do sod all, see. What with being incapacitated and all. It's *me* that runs the stall and the house."

Blowsy took a deep drag on her ever present cigarette, blowing the plume of smoke out into the air, making white, wispy rings in the process.

"Anyway, where's he gone? Been ages, he has. Can you see him at the bar from there, mate? What's your name again...John? Forget me fuckin' head if it weren't screwed on!"

Fighting my irritation towards her, I didn't have the heart to chastise the woman for her overuse of swear words, as Janice was clutching at her sides trying not to wet herself as she laughed at what her new friend had said.

"No. I can't see him. Shall I go and see where he's got to?" I asked.

"Yeah, you do that, Jack. Errr, John. Me throat's as dry as a vulture's crotch!"

Trying not to frown and fighting the urge to slap her wobbly-cheeked face, I thankfully set off looking for George as well as the drinks.

I wish the urge to get away from Blowsy hadn't been so strong and that she had been pleasant company. If I could've stayed there with her and Janice, the next phase in my life may never have begun.

Chapter Twenty-Seven

My-my. Who would have thought it of him? Who would have guessed? I had an inkling he wasn't quite right, but even I didn't suspect the real truth.

***

I made my way outside to the children's play area. I don't know why I was drawn there. Standing in the trees bordering the small park, I saw him.

George was talking to a little girl. She was a sweet wee thing. She sat on the roundabout, her hair rippling in the breeze as it spun her round and around. Large front teeth, just grown in I would say, dominated her mouth. She was giggly and happy. Just as she should be for one so young. She reminded me of Edward as a child, and it made me smile.

Standing behind this tree watching her and George, I couldn't walk away, couldn't ignore the flutter of excitement in my gut.

George threw a ball across the tarmac. A dog, I assume it was hers, bounded over to the roundabout to retrieve it. His ears flapped as he ran, and his fat Spaniel body crawled down onto the tarmac, as he used his front paws to reach the toy.

"Mister! Can you stop the roundabout? My dog's under here and I don't want him to get hurt!"

George strolled over and said, "Come here, boy!"

The dog scampered over to him.

"I got two dogs, I have!" She was still spinning on the roundabout, using her foot to propel it faster. Hair whipping her face, she lifted her small, perfect hand to move the unruly tresses out of her eyes.

"Have you? Wow, I bet he's a good doggy, just like Jasper, hmm?"

George's voice was animated. Never thought he would have it in him to sound like that. The girl looked down at the ground as she rotated. Her brown hair a mask as it fell forward. I watched, mesmerised.

"She. It was a girl dog, but she's dead now. I always say I got two dogs 'cos I forget…" Her bottom lip popped out.

"Well now, that's a shame. Do you think Jasper would like to take a little walk on the lead?"

She scuffed her shoes along the ground to stop the roundabout, her face full of concentration as she slowed. "Yeah, but…me mum, she'll be here soon and I'll get told off for talkin' to ya, 'cause you're a *stranger*."

George switched to a concerned face.

"Your mum is right, and you're a good girl for doing as she says. You stay and wait for your mum." George smiled.

I could see she was torn on whether to stay or go for a walk. She hopped off the roundabout and stood next to it, watching him walk away, unsure what to do.

"What's the time, Mister?"

George looked at his watch. "Do you know what? I'm not sure. I can't tell the time without my glasses on!" His laugh was jovial, but it sounded forced to my ears. It was hard to imagine this was the same George from inside the clubhouse.

She skipped over to him, standing a few metres away, eyes bright, face wreathed in a smile. Her ankle socks got my attention, and I took in the length of her legs in her little denim skirt.

Like a flower growing from the soil.

She reminded me of my schoolmate, Francesca, and also of my mother so many years ago when she wore the school uniform with her men friends.

"Thass alright! I can tell the time! We learned it at school!" She danced closer to George until she stood next to him, and he stooped down to show her his watch.

My heart felt like it might explode. It seemed like every beat slammed against my ribs. I felt something was amiss, that George was up to no good and I struggled with my conscience. I had done some terrible things in my life, but this seemed different somehow. Maybe it was watching someone else doing something wrong that bothered me.

"My mum'll be here soon. She's in the clubhouse, she is!"

"Well then…"

A sharp female voice broke the spell, and the little girl's hand sprang from George's arm.

"Harriet! What have I told you?"

"Oh, I'm sorry, Madam!" George turned on the charm. I was astounded that he had it in him. "Your dog's ball went under the roundabout. We got to talking about dogs, you know, and I offered to walk Jasper here, but she was a good girl, weren't you?" he glanced down at Harriet. "And she said she couldn't, because you had told her not to talk to strangers. She was just checking the time to see when you would be here."

Her mother's face softened. After all, if he *was* intent on doing wrong, who would suspect a man who looked like George? He could be anyone's Granddad.

"I'm sorry, really, but…you know, these days…" Her voice trailed off, and she looked embarrassed.

"Oh yes, I quite understand. No problem at all!" He offered a jolly grin, and then turned to Harriet, "Well, young lady. Maybe I'll see Jasper again sometime, eh? If Mummy allows it, of course."

I tilted my head in the mother's direction, smiled to myself despite my inner conflict. I *knew* what George had been up to, what he'd been planning, by instinct perhaps, and although I didn't like what I'd seen so far, I couldn't help but admire him. I knew this was what kept me watching. I wanted to see how he played it out. Blowsy's talk about George at their window came to mind, and everything fell into place.

"Are you here for much longer this evening?" This question threw George somewhat, as I could tell he had expected that his intentions had been thwarted.

"Errr, well yes, I was just about to have a rest on that seat over there."

"Well then, Harriet, you can stay with Mr umm..."

"George. George Phelps," he supplied, while slipping the dog's ball in his pocket.

"Mr Phelps," she said. "You can stay a little while then, just so you can play with Jasper. It'll save him from being cooped up in the van. Make sure you're back in the clubhouse by nine thirty, do you understand?"

Harriet began hopping from foot to foot. "Ok! Thanks, Mum!" She threw herself at her mother, and got a big hug in return.

"Be good! Oh, and thanks, Mr Phelps!" She began to back away, waving at Harriet.

"That's quite all right. And it's George."

"Ok then, George it is! My name's Sandra!"

Sandra. The stupid bitch—stupid for leaving her alone with George. Even I could see what he was about. So why didn't I say something, or step out of the bushes? Why didn't I stand up and say, "Take your child home! He's a bad man!" Half of me yearned to say it, the other half... I felt sick from the conflict within. Images of Edward at Harriet's age flickered through my mind, and I felt my fatherly instinct come to the fore. If George went too far, I decided I would stop him.

Jasper's tail wagged like mad and he strained against the lead, making Harriet's gait unsteady as she was pulled along.

"Jasper! Be a good boy. You're pulling me!"

The dog slowed a little, and the tautness of Harriet's arm eased a bit.

Walking at a slower pace, she turned to George. I followed them at a distance, taking in her features.

"Shall we throw his ball, Mister?"

"George, call me George. And yes, we can throw his ball. You go first, eh?"

He brought the ball from his coat pocket and handed it to her. Her fingers brushed his as she took it. She launched the ball, but it didn't go far, more up in the air than any great distance. The ball bounced down and rebounded up, but I could see Jasper was used to that, and waited patiently for it to come to rest.

"Your turn, Mister...George!" She was smiling, her fists clenched in excitement, legs dancing a jig.

George threw the ball a little way; Jasper retrieved it and then sat in front of Harriet. He knew the drill.

Again, Harriet threw the ball, and the dog brought it back to George.

Adopting a cricketer's stance, he propelled the sphere; lunging forward to ensure the ball went into the bushes that lined the edge of the small field next to the park.

"Awww! Look at him run, Mister George!"

She squealed in delight as the dog bounded off, ears flapping, tail waggling.

"Get it, Jasper!"

I watched as he snuffled about in the bushes, searching.

"You got it yet, boy?" George was having fun, his smile so broad that it made my cheeks hurt just looking at him. Harriet stared up at George. "You reckon we should go and help him find that ball, Harriet?"

Chapter Twenty-Eight

Would she, wouldn't she? I held my breath to see if she would indeed go with him to find that ball.

***

She put her finger to her bottom lip, frowning while she considered his question. It was Edward, Edward all over again. Did all children do this? "Yeah," she said. "Ok, 'cos I think it got lost."

She capered off, hair, that hair, streaming out behind her. Such a delightful young thing. I wondered if this child was what our daughter would have looked like, should Janice and I have ever had a girl. After Edward, no other children followed and we accepted that this was the way it would be, just the three of us. It suited us, so Janice never went to the doctors to find out if there was something wrong. Maybe if we had a daughter I wouldn't have been inclined to let George's charade continue.

I ambled after George and Harriet, glancing at my watch. Amazingly, only seven minutes had passed.

"I can't see it, Mister George!"

"Deary me, Harriet. This doggy's a silly one, isn't he? Let's follow him and see where he goes."

Again, she paused, but the dog barked excitedly, enticing her to follow. Which, of course, she did.

Jasper moved forward through the hedges, into a small glade surrounded by trees.

118

"He's funny! Don't his nose hurt when he sniffs them bits of bark on the floor?"

"Oh, I don't think so, Harriet. That's what dogs do, isn't it? Sniff about a lot! Jasper, find it. Now, boy!" George made a pretence of trying to look for the ball, and for the first time, I noticed that he was no longer limping. "I must have thrown it quite a way, eh Harriet? That ball must have bounced all the way over here!"

"Yeah, but I reckon he'll find it, 'cos he's a clever dog, right Mister George?" she said, her excitement growing.

I had seen George find the ball and put it into his pocket. He and the little girl moved further into the bushes. I heard a muffled scream, and ran over, wanting to see how far he would go. I don't know why I didn't stop it—maybe I was too wrapped up in the scene, fascinated that I had found someone that did things I hadn't even dreamed of. Trying to keep quiet, I hid in the hedge. I would stop it soon, I had to.

I couldn't see through the thick bushes, but I heard George say, "Harriet! Don't move any more, do you understand?" His voice was low, almost a growl. A strangled gasp emerged from Harriet, and I wondered what on Earth could be happening. My heart thundered at how wrong this seemed, and yet I still crouched in the hedge, unmoving. Why didn't I help her?

"Be good, and I'll let Jasper sit near you, all right?" George said.

Another gargled noise escaped Harriet.

"Good. Just. Be. Quiet…and everything will be okay!"

I heard the noises from Harriet again, and I asked myself, 'Why can't she speak? What has he done to her?' Yet still I stayed put.

"Be quiet, Harriet, there's a good girl. I'm going to take the ball out of your mouth now. Are you going to be good, and do what George tells you?" He was growling again. A lion, King of his jungle. I felt sick, was surprised at myself for feeling this way. I knew it was because I had a child of my own, that I'd be furious if someone had done this to Edward. I battled my emotions, my breathing ragged from the effort.

George spoke again, and it made me jump. "Now then, I have a nice camera here."

There were some muffled noises, like feet shuffling in undergrowth, and I heard Harriet again. She had those dry sobs that I used to get when my father scolded me as a child. If I knew her sorrow, why wasn't I helping her? If I knew how those tears felt, why wasn't I *stopping* this thing? I was confused as the rights and wrongs clashed in my mind.

"I want...me mum."

Oh God. Help me, tell me what to do. I heard the click of the camera.

Minutes passed, and then George spoke again. "All right, Harriet, we're done."

I heard a sob. It reminded me of the time Edward cried, when I heard him through the bedroom wall. Still, I stayed where I was. Still, I spent time questioning what was right and wrong and who was I to know the difference. It was best that I stayed in my hiding place.

Each time George spoke, it made me jumpy, unsettled. Was this what they called a conscience? Did I *have* one?

"It's time for you to have a little sleep. Are you tired? Would you like George to read you a story? Well, you'll be having a sleep whether you like it or not, madam!" George sounded quite affronted, spiteful.

As I listened to him, I felt that my whole equilibrium was upset.

My nerves were jarred further when George snapped, "You flinch again and I'll..."

I felt like I did as a child when Mother spoke to me in that way. I felt vulnerable and young, unsettled and so very unsure. A lump formed in my throat, and I was amazed that I actually wanted to cry.

"I want my mummy!" Harriet's wails were heartfelt and panic stricken. I dry-retched, feeling as if the whole of my stomach contents wanted out, but nothing came up. *Move, do something.* That's what I thought, that's what I wanted to do, but time was moving so fast. Just when I thought I could act, it moved on to the next scene.

"Oh dear, you really ought to shut up now. Be quiet!" George sounded angry. I could hear fresh sobs. The bile was rising into my throat, and I could feel my pulse quicken, as I too became annoyed with her cries. For someone who I found endearing such a short time ago, she really was getting on my last nerve because she was upsetting me, making me question myself, causing me confusion. I didn't know who I was, what I believed in. Or was it George who was making me feel this way? I just didn't know, didn't understand anything at that moment! Everything had been changed. The goal posts moved.

"You can't have your fucking mummy, all right? Shut the fuck up, girl. Just shut it!" I imagined him scowling, his teeth bared in anger.

I heard more scuffling noises. Was it her arms and legs flailing around? Was her torso arcing towards George as he strangled her, her lungs desperate to fill with air that would not come? Was this what was happening? I don't know. All I *did* know is that my mind was in overdrive, images flitting through at such a fast pace my head felt dizzy.

It grew quiet. I imagined Harriet limp and unmoving. It was so silent. The air seemed to have changed, gone thick with foreboding. It was then I believed she was dead.

Chapter Twenty-Nine

My veins filled with coursing blood, as if it were I who had committed the crime. I left the shelter of the hedges, the barking of Jasper now filling my ears. Absolutely no one was about.

***

I had been gone quite some time, around fifteen minutes. Sorting myself out, I went back into the clubhouse, ordered us a drink and carried them to the table on a tray, dodging dancers and small diving children.

Children. Children.

The girls who had practised the grownup dancing were still there, minus Harriet, of course. Even they were oblivious to her disappearance. I looked round for Harriet's mother, but I didn't see her. Maybe she had gone to the gaming room.

Placing the tray down on the table, I began taking the glasses from the tray, trying to slow the beat of my heart by breathing through my nose.

"Didn't you find the boring old fucker then?" Blowsy was redder than when I had left her, anger probably adding to her colour.

"Um, no, I didn't. Had a good look around, couldn't see him, so got the drinks anyway. No point in us going thirsty while we wait for him."

"Too bleeding right, Jack."

I rolled my eyes, sighing at the fact that this woman could recite all you needed to know about cleaning agents but couldn't remember a simple name like John. She must have had a problem with Janice's too, preferring to call her "love" every five minutes.

"Edward popped back at all since I was gone?" I looked at Janice as she leaned forward. She claimed her drink and sipped.

Before she could answer, Blowsy burst in with, "Yeah, wanted some more money. Going to that bowling alley he went to last night."

Janice smiled her apology, then said, "Are you all right, John?" Janice's concern touched me, as did her hand on my arm as I sat down.

"Course he's all right, love. Ain't ya, Jack?" Blowsy said. "Probably pissed off at having to look for that prat of a husband of mine. Know I would be if I were him!"

"No. It was quite all right, not to worry. I'm sure George will be back soon." I had to fight to keep my tone nice and even. "He probably just went for a walk and a bit of fresh air."

"Yeah, you're right. More like a fucking hobble than a walk though, eh? What with his bad leg!" Bawdy laughter filled our little space; other guests nodded and nudged one another, smiling at the loud mad woman having a good time on her holiday. "He'll be a good while yet then. The rate he goes!"

More whooping and slapping of her thighs followed, and I was ecstatic when George finally came back, a glint in his eye that only I would notice.

"Where the bleeding hell have you been?" Blowsy shrieked even louder, making people pause with their drinks half way to their mouths. "How dare you go fucking off like that! And you haven't even got the bloody drinks!"

George's mouth opened and closed, no sound coming out, and his eyes scanned the hall, probably for signs of Sandra, the child's mother.

"Go for a *walk* did you, George? *Children* get a bit much for you in here, did they?" I asked. He caught my glare, realizing at that moment that I knew the truth about him. He must have wondered how, but I didn't care. I felt a power in knowing his little secret.

"Errr, yes. Too stuffy in here." George gave a little cough, a clearing of his throat, his gaze still roving the multitude of faces.

"Don't blame you, George. I might go for a little stroll myself. Take a look near the *tennis courts*, you know, have a look around the site a little."

His face paled, and Blowsy noticed his pale colour.

"'Ere! Are you all right, cocker? You've gone all white!"

"Y—yes ." He stammered. "I'm fine. Just a little off colour."

"Aww! Want to go back to the van, love?"

"Yes." He looked down at his lap.

"Well fuck off then! Quite able to get yourself off over there, aren't you?" Blowsy slapped the caravan key in his hand. "Don't lock up though, will you? Can't get in if you do that and fall asleep before I get back."

George left the clubhouse. He glanced back at me as he left, the look of a caged animal on his face. I wanted to follow him, to talk to him about what had transpired, but Blowsy had requested another drink, thrusting ten pounds at me.

"May as well make them all doubles, Jack. Swear to God the bartender's watering their spirits down. Don't seem to be hitting the spot tonight, do they?"

I remember thinking briefly they had hit the spot perfectly, as she was drunk, but, decided not to say so, lest she told me to fuck off, spurring me into another murderous fit.

Twenty minutes later, Janice holding Blowsy up this time, and Edward and I walking on ahead, we made our way back to the caravans.

"'Ere! Walk me back to my van, you lot. It's as fucking dark as an African out here. What with that murder and all, I don't fancy being number two on his list!" Regina let out an obscene burp. Trying the handle on the door, and too polluted to function properly, Blowsy failed to open it. "Fuck me! Bet he's gone and locked up, the dozy bastard!"

"Here, let me." The door opened easily for me, and, leaving her teetering on the van steps, I escorted my little family to our own van.

The air was pierced with a sickening scream, followed by Blowsy waddle-swaying up the path behind us, ruddy faced and out of breath.

"Fucking Hell's bells!" Her eyes were tear-filled, her cheeks wobbling. "He's only gone and committed another bleeding killing, ain't he? Slit my George's throat!" Blubbering uncontrollably, Blowsy fumbled in her bag for her mobile telephone.

Seeing my son's shocked face, I said, "Edward, take your mother back to our van."

My tone brooked no argument. I watched as my wife and son walked quickly away, and my chest puffed with the importance of being the one in charge.

Blowsy launched herself at me, face resting on my chest, arms tugging at the back of my shirt. "And there was me, telling him to fuck off and all. Poor bloke!"

"Here, give me the phone." Janice was back to comfort her new friend, having settled Edward in the van.

While waiting for the police to arrive, I knew one thing for certain. There hadn't been another murder. George had committed suicide.

Chapter Thirty

Surprisingly, meeting with the authorities for the second time in just a few hours didn't faze me. I was amazed at my own cool demeanour.

***

Again, the police interview was easy. I had Janice and Regina as an alibi, not to mention half of the campsite had been in the clubhouse, many of whom chatted with me or said hello in the bathroom or at the bar.

Of course, it was inevitable that they would find little Harriet's body, her mother having reported her child missing just minutes after Janice's call.

I heard Harriet's mother tell the police George's name. With a bit of luck, I thought, George would get the blame for my crime too. And he did. The news swept through the camp, and I heard rumours of the investigator's theory: a paedophile had murdered the child discovered in the bushes, then took his own life.

The rest of the holiday we spent with Blowsy in tow, Janice consoling her one minute, laughing with her the next. Our statements given, we were cleared of any wrong doings depending on the outcome of the forensic reports. Free to finish our holiday, albeit with the Loud Londoner, we made the best of it we could.

"Fucking hell!" Regina cried. "What a holiday I've had, eh? Me old man has seemingly topped himself after fiddling about with a kiddie. Just shows you what you don't know about your other half, eh Janice?"

"Yes," said Janice in a strange voice, which unnerved me and made my stomach flip over.

Rolling my eyes at Edward, who then went off with his pal to play table tennis, I sifted everything through my mind. Nearby, the women continued chatting.

What a surreal time! I had experienced things I hadn't dreamed were possible. Edward had much to tell his friends when we returned home. Janice would probably keep in touch with Blowsy. I marvelled at the seemingly strong bond that had formed between them in that short space of time. I actually felt sorry in a way that she didn't live closer. But then again, she got on my nerves so much...

Returning home felt wonderful. Much as I had enjoyed the break, and boy did I ever enjoy it, it was good to be back among the familiar. It would help me get my thoughts in order.

Looking back, it was amazing that I hadn't been suspected. I did feel more than a twang of pity for Harriet's mother. Apparently, she had to be sedated when they told her Harriet had been found. Strangled and abused. It was only a slight twinge, though; I imagined myself in her position, and knew if it had been Edward... It didn't bear thinking about. My mind must be closed to the usual emotions of sorrow, conscience; for once again, I felt it was business as usual for the remainder of the holiday, as if what had happened to that little girl was a film, a movie I had seen, and wasn't real.

I did keep thinking about what I had witnessed, played it in my mind when I had an idle half hour, wondered if I would have the courage to do such a thing myself. And I knew if it was presented to me, I would. How, when I loved my own child as I did, I don't know, but something within me wanted to do what George had done, if only to see what it felt like. I must be an animal. No, not even an animal because beasts only kill their young for survival or to end an offspring's suffering. For the first time, I began to wonder if I were truly a monster.

The first night back I was unable to fall asleep. Images swirled round my brain until I felt I had to get up, make some tea with brandy in it or warm some milk, which usually settled me down.

127

Eventually, I did drop off. It must have been the police activity that caused my insomnia, the fear I had felt after killing that woman whose name was Rebecca White I later found out, a chambermaid at the site.

Something was warning me that I needed to beware.

Chapter Thirty-One

I took a break. My dreams had become weird, and I forced myself to control my urges, to hold back every time someone annoyed me, resisted hurting them. It was difficult, but I had done it before and I would do it again.

***

My resolve lasted a year or two, and then a man at a party, held at a hotel to raise funds for charity, annoyed me just a little too much that night.

I'd been a master of holding it all in, disguising what I really felt behind a happy mask. In reality, I was seething; I could've ripped off his face if I'd let the irritation within run free. He was employed at the hospital, and often annoyed me there too. I don't know why he annoyed me so. Perhaps it was the way he held himself, or that he smiled at me all the time, trying to be friendly. I didn't want to be his friend, didn't want this overly happy guy in my face and I didn't need him following me around that night. I wanted to be alone. Instead, I put on a happy face, as if everything was fine with my world and me.

I turned to him, smiling. My hands clutched my now round, distended stomach. Resembling Father Christmas, I bellowed a laugh. My shoulders shook with mirth as I found his joke funny. He warmed to me. He was drawn to me. I do not know why.

The veil slipped as I turned away. Inwardly cursing him as the stupid person I knew him to be. I went off in search of a drink; a refill that I hoped would tamper down my raging thoughts.

Drinking deep, that first swallow burned like fire. I held back a gasp, a splutter. I felt my face turning red.

"Hey up, old fella! Go down the wrong hole did it?" he said. He'd followed me after I'd turned away. To him, I was congenial. He wanted my company but didn't realise I didn't want his.

Nodding, smiling, and patting my chest, I showed him he was correct. He did not realise I was harbouring thoughts of punching him in the head for calling me old. I wondered what it would take to make him go away.

"Better now?" he asked, tilting his head to the side, which enabled him to see my face, as I was hunched over still coughing.

I remember clearing my throat. "Uh, yes. Yes, thank you indeed." I turned from him again.

He scooted round to face me, but he didn't see that my features had become strained. I may have been grinning, but it was the grin of the annoyed.

"As long as you're sure!" he said.

I was going to place my hand over his face and shove him over backwards if he didn't shut his mouth and leave me alone. I had the urge to stamp on his head after he hit the floor until his skull popped open and his brains splattered on the tiles.

"Yes, yes! Quite sure!" I replied, clearing my throat noisily to let him know my airway was clear; that there was nothing for him to worry about, so now go away and leave me alone.

I offered him another smile, but it nearly killed me.

I walked away purposely towards the toilets. I felt the need to splash water on my face and dash away the thoughts racing through my mind. I needed to be alone, to calm the feelings I held inside.

I leaned over the sink, dousing my face in the cold droplets and shaking my head to clear it of the demonic images it held. I revelled in being alone; I rarely was. I jumped when I heard him speak.

He'd followed me again to check on me.

"Hey! There you are! Feeling more chipper?"

Keeping my eyes closed as I straightened, I reached blindly for the blue paper towels. I dried off my face, and when I opened my eyes, he stood watching me, entranced.

I turned towards him. "I'm feeling a little off colour, actually."

My breathing was laboured, as if I couldn't catch my breath.

"Oh, well! That's not good is it? We can't have that!" He reached to take my elbow. "Let's go out onto the terrace. You'll benefit from the cool fresh air."

Feeling cornered, my gaze darted from side to side looking for an escape route. Trying to make my thoughts disperse, I struggled to appear calm. He was oblivious to my raging internal war.

I didn't want my elbow tugged, but he didn't know that. I was far too polite to pull away. At that moment, it struck me as odd that I could be so polite and murderous at the same time. I let him lead me through the crowd and on outside. I leaned against the wrought iron fencing that edged the terrace, my elbows resting on the ledge, head hanging low between my arms. I heard myself taking in deep breaths.

"My! You *are* a bit under the weather, aren't you?"

I felt his concern, but he was irritating me beyond measure. When other people apart from Janice, Edward or my father showed me concern it irked me beyond reason, because it wasn't *her*, it wasn't Mother. My mind was fogging, thoughts becoming unclear, fuzzy around the edges, blurred. The common denominator of my mental images was that they all included hurting him, this man who insisted on being so *nice*.

I felt hemmed in, as I rested my left flank against the railing in the corner, and he was on my other side with his hand on my back. His upper body leaned over to his right, trying to see my face, to get a measure of how I was feeling.

I felt trapped again, wanted him to leave. He was invading my space as well as my mind. I brought my body upright, knowing that if I didn't get away from him soon, I would burst. I wanted to run. If I had space between him and me, my mind would quiet.

He took a step back and removed his hand from the small of my back.

"Do you need a drink of water?" he asked as I got a pressed handkerchief from my top pocket, snapping it out of its folds with a crack in the air like a pellet gun. His brow furrowed as he watched me mop mine.

I turned to him. Smiled. "No. No, thank you."

"If you would please excuse me," I said, knowing he watched me as I dashed off through the crowds, moving people out of my way by gripping their shoulders, pushing them aside. He was probably wondering what on earth could be wrong, but I didn't care. I had to get away from him.

I chose the steps and raced down them; the confines of the elevator would have driven me insane. I felt the need to run as far away from mankind as possible, to prevent myself from hurting someone.

That need had been in me for many years, something I had learned to live with, the majority of the time stifling it, keeping it at bay. For quite some time the urges had engulfed me, wrapping around me like the pastry on a sausage roll.

I made it to the car park, head roaring, lungs bursting, face sweating. I could feel the hair on my head standing up in their follicles; the soft down on the nape of my neck rising. I stood and took deep breaths, trying to steady my thumping heart, concentrating on the sound of my breathing and shut out the pounding in my ears.

Calmer, I strolled to a cluster of trees, leaning against one while my battle slowly receded.

"Hey there!"

He had pursued me to check that I was all right. *Again.* He had no idea the struggle I'd been having. My blood pressure rose again, the pounding in my ears returned louder than ever, my heart pumping so fiercely that it was a wonder it didn't pop with the force.

I turned to him as his hand touched my arm. He didn't see my fist coming. He had no clue what he had started.

Mercifully, he was out like a light.

I dragged him deeper into the cluster of trees, and then acted on my earlier impulse and stamped on his head with both feet until he didn't move anymore. I looked down at his broken face and felt no remorse, triumphant that I had given in to my calling. I walked across the grass, scuffing my shoes as I walked to rid them of his mess. Blood had spattered the bottoms of my trousers and I felt disgust, wanting to change my clothes as soon as possible. I wondered briefly if Janice would notice the blood, question me as she did with the wet clothes that time. Maybe I could get home without anyone noticing them, wash them before Janice spied the mess.

My chest swelled and I muttered to myself that people really should learn to read body language. People needed to learn to respect the wishes of others.

I wondered when the rage would return. When the next person would pursue me and not take the hint when I wished to be left alone.

Having these rages has its perks. And he had been one of them.

Chapter Thirty-Two

To walk away unfazed from such a scene may amaze you. I felt relief, like a burden had been lifted, that I was able to shirk the chains that bound me so easily. Unfettered, I walked home.

***

Hopefully, I hadn't been seen. Should I get caught, I did not want to bring trouble upon Janice. I cursed myself for giving in to my urges so easily. Maybe I was out of control? What the hell was wrong with me?

As was my luck on these occasions, Janice had been unable to attend the party. She often had to work second or third shift at the hospital. Edward had stayed with Father, so going home to an empty house was a bonus. I scraped my shoes clean and washed and dried my clothing before anyone else came home.

The next evening, the news channels reported my crime.

"Oh my God! Isn't that the party you went to, John?"

I looked up from my poetry book, knowing full well it was the same party, having been listening to the news whilst pretending to read. Shocked, Janice stared at the TV. When she looked at me, she wore a horrified expression. The distrust in her eyes nearly knocked me out of my chair. How had it come to this? My wife, looking at me like that? Was my carefully erected guise slipping? Did I think I was behaving normally when in fact I wasn't? I must keep calm, appear *normal.*

"Hmm?" I said.

Best to feign nonchalance. Inside, I worried about Janice truly realising the truth about me, but at the same time, I felt gleeful that my deed had made the big news and not just the local. I had to try quite hard not to laugh.

"That murder! Look! It happened at the hotel you were at the other night!"

"Good grief! So it did!" I hoped that I sounded genuinely shocked.

We listened for a few minutes, watched the news reporter standing just in front of the trees where I had been, telling us in his sombre voice of the tragedy, the horror of this senseless killing.

It was a bloody tragedy that the man had annoyed me. He got what he deserved. He wouldn't be bothering anyone with his overly concerned manner again. He should have left me alone and not been caring towards me. Only Janice, Edward and my father were permitted to care for me, love me.

"I might have to start worrying about you, John!"

"Hmmm?" I broke my gaze from the television, "Why's that then?"

I really hadn't expected what she said next. It had never entered my head that if Janice suspected the truth, it wouldn't be long before the police did the same. I realized that my name might be linked to yet another murder with me as a statement giver. Coincidence? No, no one would ever believe that.

"Well," Janice said. "Every time there's a murder or someone's hurt, you know, Lucy and her mum, those holiday murders, you've been out on your own! I should be scared witless by rights!"

She was smiling. I knew she was joking, *hoped* she was joking, but all the same, my blood ran cold. My stomach felt as though it was shrivelling up, the icy hand of fear squeezing it tight.

Masking my thoughts, I remember the deep breath I took that helped me say, "Janice! What a thing to say! Makes me look awful!"

I laughed too, got up, and stepped into the kitchen, shouting in a casual tone, "Do you want a coffee, love?"

"Please." The room was quiet for a moment, then she said, "I was only messing about you know, John."

135

"I know, love. Whoever the murderer is must have a pretty good reason to kill someone."

Janice got up, leaning against the kitchen doorframe, arms crossed over her stomach. "You can't seriously mean that?"

I smiled, pouring the water into our cups. "Of course I don't mean it! Was trying to lighten the mood, that's all. Murder isn't something I'd choose to talk about."

Oh, but it was. If only there was someone out there to talk about it to. Someone I could trust, and share experiences with.

"I'll agree with that," Janice said. "Anyway, this has reminded me to ring Regina."

Janice and Blowsy spoke to one another frequently on the telephone, sometimes in whispers. Once, Janice even left the room, trailing the telephone cord behind her like a long mouse's tail to sit on the stairs. She spoke so quietly that even my straining to hear revealed nothing.

Watching her take her coffee to the sofa and pick up the phone, I knew Janice would probably talk to Blowsy for quite some time, so I pointed to the ceiling, letting her know I'd be upstairs, using my binoculars.

Stargazing calmed me.

It never entered my head that my wife could possibly be discussing the murders and me with the loud Londoner. I didn't suspect it at all.

Chapter Thirty-Three

Things have a habit of springing up on you. I always believed that the police would one day bring me up short, but no, no, it wasn't them at all...

***

Time passed, and Father was getting on in years. I noticed his back was a little stooped, his hair thinning, and white now instead of grey. Lively enough, though. I didn't think I had reason enough to worry but still, it took me by surprise. How had I not noticed the years passing, aging his skin, making his eyelids droop, his mouth turn down slightly?

I shoved these thoughts from my mind as an unreasonable urge overcame me to run into his arms. I watched him on the bank, holding his fishing rod.

"Everything ok, John?"

He didn't look at me, but kept his eyes firmly on the water, waiting for any sign that a fish was close.

"Fine, Dad, fine. Edward's enjoying work now, and college, you know..."

"Good lad. He'll learn all he needs to know if he sticks at it. Plumbing may not be the most glamorous of apprenticeships but there'll always be blocked drains. He'd do well to remember that. Always be a job in plumbing. Like your electrician, they're always needed. Get away with charging the earth too, on those call outs they do."

"He knows all that, Dad," I replied, sitting down next to him. I fiddled with a blade of grass, picking at it with my finger and thumb, slightly annoyed with this beloved man, who felt the need to comment on Edward as if I hadn't had the foresight to talk to my own son about his career.

"He's a good lad, is our Edward."

"He is that," I said.

That was the last conversation we ever shared. That night, after I had walked away, going home to my family, Father had climbed into bed and died in his sleep. He died of natural causes—not by my hand. Even I wouldn't stoop that low.

The passing of my father didn't hit me properly for quite some time. I think the part of my brain that processes hurt and sadness had shut down, or maybe I just didn't want to believe that my hero was gone.

It wasn't until Janice and I cleared out the cabin that the grief slammed into me. Seeing things from my childhood that he had kept, things I had forgotten about had me choking on my tears.

Crouched in a ball on the floor, I sobbed. Janice kneeled next to me with her hand upon my back; unable to soothe the pain I was feeling. A void opened up within me, creating such a hollow that I could feel my whole self falling into the chasm, swallowing up my very essence.

I don't want to write about that anymore. It hurts too much.

I didn't care about anything much after that. Not Edward or Janice, my job, or myself. Depression consumed me at that time, so overwhelming that I sometimes didn't realise a whole week had passed.

I'd go to Father's grave to tell him of my troubles, hoping he hadn't become aware in the afterlife of all I had done. Somehow though, I didn't feel remorse for my past, but I just didn't want Father knowing about it except from my mouth. I had to be the one to explain it to him one day. I wanted to sit on the newly grown grass upon his grave and relate my past. Only I could make him understand my reasons.

Maybe in the next world they could explain it all, make him see...

My marriage began to suffer. I became moody after Edward moved out to live with friends in a flat, going to college once a week and work the rest. I found it hard to believe that seventeen years had passed since his birth. Where had the time gone?

Janice began staying with Blowsy in London most weekends. It was her way of escaping my bad temper and complete silences, I suppose. I didn't really know for sure as we didn't discuss it much. I had constructed an impenetrable brick wall. We had drifted apart, and at that time, I didn't seem to care, so consumed was I with my own importance, my own grief.

She rang me one Sunday afternoon to say she wasn't coming back, except to pick up some clothes and bits and pieces, before moving to London near Blowsy. I had always hated Blowsy, but at that moment, I despised her the most that I ever had, and blamed her for luring my wife away, encouraging her to leave me during those long phone calls. I should have put a stop to it, to their friendship, and talked to Janice more myself, but I didn't. I only had myself to blame.

I remember at the time feeling that I should be fighting, should have strived to correct the wrongs. After all, Janice was my one and only love. Wasn't she? Or did I love my inner devil more? Did I *really* know what love was?

I said, in a frantic bid to salvage our marriage and right the wrongs, "But Janice! What's happened to us? I thought we were ok!"

"We were, John, but you've changed. You're not the same person that I married." She sounded distant, hard and cold. I was too late. Too bloody late.

I felt my world caving in, knew if I didn't try to persuade her I'd be useless on my own. I'd never be whole again. "We all change as we age, Janice, you know that! Come on! Come home, I'll stop being so moody; I'll try to be how I was. We can't just let this thing go. Please, love. *Please* come back."

The lump in my throat threatened to cut off my air supply. My head spun. Thoughts of being without her made me feel physically sick. I was floundering, scared of being by myself, wondering if I could be like I was before for her. God only knew how I would be if she stayed with Regina, if she didn't come home. Home wouldn't *be* home without Janice. "Oh God, help me. Tell me what to say, what to do!"

But I knew she didn't want to make it work, nor did she want to understand my desperation. Janice just accepted what I'd said with indifference. Looking back, it was probably for the best. She would never be tainted by me should I ever get caught. She wouldn't have to admit ever having known me once the divorce came through and she had returned to her maiden name.

The cabin was still empty, my father having bought it many years ago, leaving it to me to do with what I would. So I moved there, taking what furniture would fit, taking time to heal myself within the familiar confines of those walls.

I never again visited the house I had shared with Janice and Edward. Nor did I see Janice for many years, until Edward got married. She was a new person, alien, a stranger. Re-married to a nice looking man who appeared to worship her. While I had mourned the loss of our marriage, admitting she deserved better than I, she had gone and found just that. Someone who didn't put her at risk. A part of me wanted to believe that no one, *no one* would love Janice more than I did, but time makes you accept things, and if I loved her as I thought I did, I would never have committed those crimes.

Edward visited once a month, and we fished in the stream like my father and I used to do. It brought back painful memories, but it also helped to ease some of the pain I was feeling. Edward had become distant with me since his mother and I parted ways. Perhaps he too had noticed the change in me. So preoccupied was I in teaching people a lesson for slighting my loved ones, I did not realise that I had been neglecting them as well.

Still, I clung to the times Edward came to see me, revelled in our shared conversations, even if they were a little stilted. It must have been hard on the lad to not mention his mother. After all, he saw her quite often; she was a big part of his life. I pitied myself, but felt sorrow for Edward. What a mess it had all become. I felt as lonely as the boy I used to be. Father and Janice were gone, and I rarely saw my son. Perhaps I had got what I deserved.

I stayed in most nights, until one time I couldn't bear looking at the walls any longer. I decided it was time to get out, and I made my way over to the pub where everyone met after work.

Chapter Thirty-Four

I felt a bit anxious as I walked into The Blue Star. I hadn't been here in a long time. First, my father died, my marriage broke up, and then I just lost the heart to go out anywhere. It took a lot to persuade myself to go there that night, but there are only so many times you can put life off.

***

I was greeted with smiles and slaps on the back, and many a "How are you, mate? Long time no see in here!" and the apprehension slid away somewhat. For a while, I slipped into the old mode. I felt wanted and cared for, like my life hadn't been a waste of time after all.

That first pull on my pint went down like liquid gold. You can't beat a lager from the glass. Cans just don't taste the same, and I knew that I'd sunk enough of them in the past three months. Even the froth on my upper lip tasted like copper coins, a taste to savour.

Everyone was smiling as they dug out change for the pool table. The jukebox was playing a tune by Lenny Kravitz, but the title's slipped my mind. I stood watching the others, a grin on my face. It felt good to be home.

"Oi, John! Fuckin' John! Where you been, mate?"

I turned to see Frank, an old work pal, who I hadn't seen since Janice upped and left. Frank's the type of friend you only see in the pub or at work, he doesn't pop round for chats.

142

"Frank! How're you doing?"

"Fine, John, fine! You?"

I smacked him on the back, and he grasped my hand with both of his, pumping it up and down, his eyes showing how glad he was to see me, his smile as wide as Blowsy's backside. Thinking of her made me grit my teeth and I paused slightly before saying, "I'm great, mate, great! You?"

He'd expected that answer so I gave it, and he ruffled the front of my hair, pointed his finger at me, as if he were cocking a gun, and winked.

"Smilin' as always, John! Not a care in the world, that's me!"

That was when the truth started to settle around me like a soft mantle gently cloaking me. Wrapping itself around my person, I shuddered, and inside my mind, everything turned stale and mouldy. I kept the smile plastered on my face, and nodded at Frank before taking a swig of my beer. He walked off to grab his friend, Toby, round the neck from behind, and I smiled and laughed, knowing I didn't really find it funny at all—just sad.

Hell! I would have loved to be able to walk around in my life and not have a care in the world again. I looked at Frank and wondered just what was really going on inside his mind. Some people look so sad and upset you have to wonder what's happened to them, and others, like Frank, walk round laughing and grinning, seemingly without a care in the world. I tried to be like that at work, to smile and have people think everything was okay. Well, it bloody well wasn't okay, but I didn't want to go down that road that night.

I mentally shook the cloak from my shoulders, but caught myself before someone noticed my movements and wondered what I was doing. I pulled on my pint, a long soothing gulp, and grimaced in pleasure as it hit the spot, which then reminded me of Blowsy and that holiday. Draining the last quarter, I turned towards the bar, and Des, the landlord, had already got his hand out, ready to refill.

"Same again, John?"

I nodded and took a fresh mouthful, feeling it slide down. Standing at the bar alone, looking round at all my work mates, shooting pool, throwing some darts, smoking, and whacking their thighs when a joke or anecdote made them laugh till they nearly choked. I realised that I didn't fit in, never had, and the cloud descended once again.

I told myself off. Bloody hell, man! Pull yourself together. Your workmates would love the single life you've got, judging by the way they pull apart their wives.

I heard their voices becoming more ribald, even though they were only on their second pint, and I glanced up to look at the lads, unaware I'd been picking at my fingernails, head bowed.

"Hey, John! Come over here, you boring fucker!"

It was Frank again. Everyone else laughed, looking my way for a second, and then continuing with their pool and darts. I wanted to be over there with them, but the bonhomie I felt upon entering that place had vanished, and I felt as drained as the pint glass in my hand.

After another refill, I turned away from the lads and looked at myself in the mirror behind the bar. My life felt over. Not much to look forward to except going to work and Edward's visits. I needed my hair cut. It looked greasy and unkempt, even though I had spruced myself up before coming out, which had been a struggle in itself.

It was at that point that the voice in my head piped up, and I really had to concentrate to shut it out. I didn't want to listen to it that night. It had been my constant companion forever and I was sick of hearing its voice, winding me up like a coil, until I snapped, and then laughing at me when I came undone, and everything unravelled.

I thought I had sorted out the depression by having the courage to go to the pub that night. I knew when it was going start, and I thought I knew how to kick its backside and make it get the hell out of my life. The trouble was that the voices and the depression were clever, and they'd catch me unawares. I'd been down the bottom of that proverbial well with only a pinprick of light at the top to strive towards. I'd decided to climb out of that well that night and over the top into the sunlight. My fingers may have bled from the effort, my heart a little battered from beating too heavily for too long, but I'd got out of that cabin and back out into the world.

I didn't want it to hit me like that again. Still, it was there, tapping on my door, asking to come inside. And I was angry, angry that it was knocking, and angry at letting myself be angry at the fact that I wanted to give in to it. It confused me into thinking I was angry at the anger, and then it slipped in un-noticed and settled down for the duration.

I pulled myself out of my reverie and tried to think of something funny or amusing as I looked round the bar, but there was nothing funny about watching grown men make prats of themselves, getting drunker as the night wore on. Voices were growing louder, and I had to stifle the urge to bolt out the front door. That cloak had a lot to answer for, and I gritted my teeth, the muscles in the side of my face twitching as I tried to control my mood. Regardless, it controlled me.

I shook away the depression like rain off a dog's back, telling myself there were worse things in life I could be enduring. In fact, I had already endured some such things like various forms of abuse, being treated like dirt and the lack of money. We'd been so poor that I once watched Janice scrape peas from the shelf of the freezer to add a little taste to the rice and tin of chopped tomatoes she'd made for tea. And then watched her face as Edward complained that it tasted like dirt, which in turn had made me weep in private for at least she had tried to feed us. I was ashamed that I couldn't offer them more. Our wages from the hospital didn't pay well, so we had always struggled.

I could hear the lads talking about cajoling me, but from the corner of my eye, I saw Toby put a hand on Frank's arm to stop him.

"Leave him, mate," Toby said. "Let him enjoy his pint in peace. Got things on his mind, man."

Yes. Things on my mind. I wanted this miasma to leave me alone, wanted to feel alive again. Yet those creeping fingers of depression still touched me, stroked me, causing a false sense of security.

I was feeling very low at that point and the sound of my work mates having a good time was only making it worse. I didn't want to be here, propping up the bar when I may as well be crashed on the sofa with a can of beer in my hand and a cigarette in the other, watching film after film, in the hopes it would make the loss of my father and Janice more tolerable.

And to make it worse, that voice came back.

The bar and its sounds seemed so far away. I'd let the cloak shroud me yet again, and I didn't even feel angry about it, just sad and despondent. I placed my empty glass on the bar, lifted a hand in farewell to Dan, and left the pub, not even looking in the lads' direction.

I was weary of fighting off yet another day of depression. I really wanted to shout in anger, but I didn't have the energy.

I stood breathing in the cold night air, filling my lungs with its icy coldness, trying to revive the lethargy that had settled within my body. I wanted the sharp breeze to sweep away the utter desolation I felt in my mind, the despondency. But it was useless.

I trudged home, wanting nothing more than to sleep it all away.

Chapter Thirty-Five

I awoke the next day, the birds twittering in the trees. The birdsong made me think of Twinkle and the times we shared. It seemed to cast a balm over me.

***

Watching the fingers of sunlight filter through the curtains, I seemed to sense a change, as though the shroud that had finally encompassed me for the past few years had lifted. For the first time in ages, I felt I could get up and face the day ahead.

People at work noticed the change and went out of their way to say hello again instead of avoiding me. I must have been a surly, unpleasant fellow, though I tried to appear jolly, and I told myself that no longer would I let that cursed cape of depression wrap itself around my shoulders again.

Today was a new beginning. I could think of no better way to begin than by listening to my inner demons. I was ready to do my best, to do what I was good at doing. It was all I had left in my life.

Memories of my baby brother were finally coming back to haunt me. Maybe I did have a heart after all because the previous night's dream came to me then, at first a small frisson of what had played before my closed eyelids, and then the whole thing...I remembered, saw it all...

In the dream, my guts ached from retching, and my ribs were sore. My eyes stung from so many tears. Father would have said I had frog eyes from crying and the "hicclepuffs" from sobbing. I knew if I tried to speak, nothing coherent would emerge from my lips.

My heart beat so wildly I feared it would burst out of my chest. It thumped so insistently, so *hard*, that it hurt. I had the sense that someone would soon get hurt.

I washed my face with cold water, swiping across my cheeks with my palms in a soothing motion. If only it were as easy to smooth away this empty void.

I've never felt pain like this before. I feel like I'm going to split open. It hurts so badly that I want to die. It grows worse and worse. It doesn't let up. It's taking me over.

In my dream, the clothes pegs I had taken with me to the alleyway had come in handy. There was a baby, newborn, still bloodied from birth and I hacked through the cord with a pair of nail scissors. It wailed and waved its limbs. I tried not to look, but curiosity got the better of me. Once the cord was cut, it filled its lungs and let out an almighty shriek like a banshee wail. Red faced, fists bunched, hammering the air like a boxer at a punching bag. Angry. Probably cold. So ferocious looking.

The pain started again in my head. The baby was still squealing on the tarmac, its cries getting louder by the minute. I would have to shut it up.

Crouching over the tiny body I lifted it up. I felt inexperienced, my hold was unsteady; its head flopped back as if it were mounted on elastic. Arms and legs kicked and punched. I swaddled it in a blanket and placed it atop a pile of black bin liners full of refuse next to the industrial sized wheelie bin. Someone would find it; I wanted it to be found. Thankfully, the screaming had died down into a whimper, easing the ache in my brain. It must have indeed been cold. Maybe being wrapped up in the blanket gave it a feeling of security.

I took one last look at the baby. I felt nothing for that little person. I poured lighter fluid onto some papers, and set them alight with the flick of a match. A wind started up. Garbage from the pile began to scatter. It danced in the breeze towards the flames, where it too ignited.

It began to cry again. Fidgeting on its bed of rubbish until a toilet roll plopped from the refuse and rolled towards the pyre. Flames grabbed the new addition and streaked along the length of the tissue, igniting the swaddled child's blanket.

I'm running. Out of breath, lungs bursting, I run from the alley towards the woods.

I saw Harriet there, dead on the ground. Was she watching from Heaven, angry at what I had done, as I looked at her closed eyelids? Was her spirit yearning to smite me for not saving her from George?

I didn't know. I didn't care. I didn't want to be in the woods. Harriet is gone, as was George's intention. She paid the price of being young, of wearing knee-high socks and a gymslip.

I looked down at her. Leaves, curled from being brittle and dry, intertwined in her hair. Tresses splayed out like a fan, muddied and unkempt. Fingers curled palm wards, her nails broken and filled with dirt. Pink coat concertinaed to the waist.

Legs, bare.

Shoes, lost.

Still I gazed, snapshot images indelible on my brain, the spool of negatives stored.

Did her eyelashes flicker or was it merely the breeze, brushing over pale cheeks, her lips tinged blue?

Grey. She was grey.

Light began filtering through the trees, as the early sun rose.

Stiff, I rose from my night vigil, bones creaking. Home beckoned to me and I was tired. I looked down one last time before leaving her with the chambermaid, who had appeared out of nowhere beside Harriet.

Children of the forest.

I have no idea why I dream these things. Perhaps visions of my past deeds were mixing together to make one fresh new experience. What I do know, though, is that it enlivened me, gave me a new burst of energy. The lethargy was gone. I was ready to begin again.

Chapter Thirty-Six

Sometimes workdays drag. Especially when you have something more exciting to look forward to once the day is over. An irritating person who worked in the café needed a lesson. And I decided I would be her teacher.

***

Leaving work, I felt almost jaunty. I felt so light and free of burdens that I could have skipped. I only had myself to answer to now and I doubted that I would question myself too closely. I wanted to do things on a whim, just get up and do it, not think about it too much, and see where my fancies took me.

Jung worked in the hospital cafeteria. The woman irritated me constantly and was always smiling at me, her squinty Asian eyes disappearing. She made the hairs on my neck stand on end. Everyone else seemed to find her lovely. I, however, did not. She annoyed me with her incessant questions too.

"You not wan chips wi tha?" she'd ask, peering at me with her black, almond-shaped eyes. "You wan some ketchup?"

No, I just wanted her to leave me alone, to order my own chips, pick up the ketchup bottle myself without her help. Some days I could totally ignore her. Other times I would pretend she hadn't spoken, but for the past few months I had put up with her grating queries and I didn't want to do that anymore. Why should she care if I wanted ketchup or salt and vinegar? What was it to her? Why did she smile at me as if she cared for me, was concerned about *me*?

I hate it when strangers are capable of something my mother was not, and it results in an uncontrollable urge within. I feel it building, growing, festering like a cancer, making me want to strike them, kill them.

I knew her shift ended half an hour after mine. She would go and eat some leftover sandwiches in the park by the duck pond as was her habit, her back to the bushes as she sat tossing bread to the drakes and smiling so that her eyes narrowed even more.

So I'd collected my heavy bag, slung it over my shoulder and made my way to those bushes to wait for her.

Although I was forty-years-old and sitting in a bush, at that moment, I felt like ten again. The familiar angst made me giddy and hyper, wanting to laugh out loud, but of course I couldn't.

I remember thinking that I couldn't keep getting away with this. Surely the authorities were looking harder to find me. Who knew? And of course, once again, I didn't care. Everything fell into place when I felt like this. The shackles of real life didn't affect me; I was John Brookes The Unstoppable.

How naïve could I get?

She came along then, settled herself down on the bench, the moon casting its image on the lake's surface. We had both worked the afternoon shifts that day. Her black, short hair sprung up in tufts and I had the urge to jump out from the bush and pull it, but I held back. Doing that would spoil the best part.

The bushes I'd hidden in had a small clearing inside, large enough to do what I wanted. Higher than a six-foot man, the leaves created a canopy, the moonlight filtering through enough so that I could see what I was doing.

I shifted my weight a little, winced as the leaves rustled somewhat, watched her head turn slightly as she registered the sound, shrugging it off as a night animal or bird behind her.

Stupid girl.

My adrenalin was pumping now. She threw the bread to the ducks, who seemed oblivious to her even being there, probably nesting somewhere on the island in the centre of the lake.

Water plopped as the fishes came up for the spoils and the bass entered my thoughts, making me highly aroused as the images of my youth filled my mind. My erection strained against my jeans so that I had to move slightly to ease the uncomfortable feeling.

Again, her head turned, and again, she shrugged.

I lunged.

She screamed as I yanked at her short hair and stuffed an old sock into her open mouth. Grabbing her by the tops of her arms, I shoved her backwards into the bush. Her legs scrabbled for purchase on the gravely pathway, feet digging into the damp earth in the small clearing, hands clawing at mine.

Shoving her down on the ground, I picked up my mallet, and smacked her on the head with it. She landed, face up, legs bent at the knee, turned to a forty-five degree angle to her torso, her arms upwards, face blood-smeared, eyes glazed and unseeing.

A quick death, but I didn't care. I hadn't finished yet.

Something startling came to mind then, a TV image I must have buried long ago as soon as I had seen it as a child. As young as I was then, I probably couldn't comprehend what had happened.

I based my actions on this movie now. I peered down at the Asian cadaver, bringing to mind what the actor in the film had done: he'd chopped his victim up in a frenzy, hacked away at his lifeless form, and beat him upon the head with a mallet. I relished in the feelings this scene gave me.

I wanted to be that man in the film, that killer. I even wanted to look like him. I remember standing transfixed, staring at the TV screen as a child thinking, *this guy is so cool!*

First, taking my axe, I raised it above my head with both hands, bringing it down in one swift motion, trying to sever her leg at the thigh but it took several more hacks before I got through just the muscle. The force within me had woken up, taking over my everyday senses, urging me to strike this body anywhere, everywhere. I grinned wider, bringing images to mind of pig carcasses hanging in butcher's windows, cuts of meat in polystyrene packages.

Feeling tired, I tossed the axe aside and reached for my mallet, which brought forth additional movie memories, the actor luring a man into the forest, slicing the skin off his torso with a knife. Me, watching, ever engrossed, unable to tear my gaze away from the television (or movie) screen. I must have been so small, but I suddenly remembered it as if it were yesterday. The crackle of dead wood and leaves beneath the character's feet as he slashed at the victim's chest in glorious motions, my tiny heart beating wildly at the images. I could hear the background music in my head, building up to a crescendo as the actor killed and hacked and slashed and hurt and I was a brave boy. I didn't cry. Not once did I cry, I remembered that then.

I grunted, gripping the mallet with both hands until my palms felt sore.

Time to perform like that actor.

Chapter Thirty-Seven

I needed to work out what I should do, where I should go from here. Whether I should continue or go down a completely different track.

***

To sit and write this down has been more than beneficial to me. Piecing together my past in the best way I know how, I have been able to relive my past, knowing I cannot ever commit such acts again. There is still a way to go, still something I have yet to tell you.

From where I am, leaning on my patio table while I write I can see the step that I had sat on the night Mother came looking for Father. see through the kitchen window and in my mind's eye I once more glimpse the images of that time.

I see the stream to my right, hear it bubbling over the stones and pebbles, the birds cawing, flying free and without burdens. The only worry they have is to find food for their young, bits of dried grass and suchlike to build their nests. If they are lucky they'll find a dry and safe roof to nest in.

Gone are the days when little John Brookes and his cat stalked that garden for their operations. After I moved into the cabin with Father, Twinkle died a couple of years later.

I suppose I feel a little sad for the boy I once was. If other parents had raised me, if I'd received the love I deserved from my mother instead of being shunned I may have acted differently. But then again, if something is in you, it's in you, and there's nothing any of us can

154

do about it. The urges could have been held back but being weak-willed I could never ignore them for long.

Ahead of me is a row of trees that border the farm next door where sheep graze in the field, bleating to one another about the length of the grass or whatever it is that sheep talk about. To my left, next to the cabin is the pathway to the road.

A road runs past the front of the cabin, many vehicles trundle along it at all hours of the day, though you get used to the noise. Years ago that road used to be more of a lane.

Behind me is a fence that lines the edge of this property where a big, new house has been built; the nouveau riche owners have not moved in yet, so I still get my small amount of privacy. That will soon change, of that I have no doubt.

So, I have scenic views; I have a nice adequate home. I can scribble in my notebook to my heart's content, pouring out my life and drinking it down, much like that bottle of red wine there on the table with the glass empty beside it.

Should I get some more wine and replenish my glass? Do I tell you that last little bit about me before I lay down my pen and close the cover of my notebook?

I suppose I should, really.

I needed to do something different. Something that I hadn't done before, but would give me the same buzz, that same feeling of being in control, exalting in my acts.

Chapter Thirty-Eight

Again the dreams plagued me. Thinking about George and changing my course accordingly had been my downfall. Dreams sent me messages, and when I woke, I was always chilled, knowing exactly what my fate would be.

***

There are times when I have flown through this life, swiftly and with no hesitations, spread my wings as wide as they would reach, and pushed through the days with a puffed chest. Exalted by my learning, gaining wisdom through my mistakes, learning knowledge through the error, I flew.

Times have passed where I've sucked the very life from Janice, whom I professed to love. I took everything she had had to offer and dashed it back into her face like so much refuse. I toyed with her emotions to the point of her shedding tears, her face turned towards me, her eyes pleading.

To witness the joy of others, and then bring their emotions crashing down, I took a perverse satisfaction in watching them crumble beneath my wrath. It gave me pleasure. A spectre of a smile brushed my lips when I observed the pain that I have caused by a mere word or action.

Yet still people chose to be in my company, fluttering around me like so many moths to the flame—a kamikaze pilot, flying headlong into the depths of the fire. I marvel at their stupidity. I suppose they

156

can't be blamed for wanting to be with me, after all, they thought I was a nice guy.

Abusing a person emotionally, mentally and physically brings pleasure to my soul. I can appear innocent, gaining their trust before causing them hurt and pain. I can smile showing perfect teeth, and tilt my head at an angle that belies the fact that I'm as hard as granite inside. The light of a smile does not reach my eyes, but they do not see that. They see my lips stretch and assume I'm happy, that I'm normal. Undertones of malice lace my voice sometimes when I speak to people, yet they do not hear it

Becoming lackadaisical in my ministrations, the façade I had so carefully crafted slipped away as stones down a cliff. My hold upon their minds and emotions loosened as they grew away from me, and as my grasp became less sure their grip on life grew firmer. For them, realisation burst upon their irises, their retinas grabbing the light, their pupils retracting with the view that was before them. They saw my lack of care and decided they didn't need me, they would move on.

I realise times change, and tables become turned, I just didn't expect it to happen to me. My flight through the days became laboured, and my wings seemed clipped, less agile in their movements. I no longer felt free to do as I pleased but hemmed in by the constraints of my marriage, by responsibilities. When me and Janice parted, when Edward went on to live his own life I felt the currents become colder as I flew through *my* life, and my chest deflated, I felt less sure of myself and got depressed. My beak opened wide as I squawked my protest into the deaf night, the stars and moon the only thing that heard my sobs of loneliness. The sins I committed against others were returned upon me by karma. I felt shattered of heart, and broken of spirit as I tried to claw my way back into enjoying my life as I once had.

At one time I was convinced people stared right through me, their orbs of sight piercing my own eyes with invisible lightening bolts, and my cheeks would stain with the flush of the abashed. I felt people were beginning to see me for what I was—that they had begun to guess what I had done. People's heads changed direction, and if I spoke to them they would make out they had missed my approach, hadn't seen me coming. Silence abounded as I drew near to friends, and their conversations halted or stilted, making me feel excluded. Exclusion did not sit well, yet I was unable to grasp the vigour that had once belonged to me, enabling me to strike back at them with my vengeance.

The fight poured from me in my depressive period as milk from a broken bottle, making me feel defeated. Without those whom I had control over I had nothing. Shoulders turned, people turned their backs on me. Everywhere I went I received the same response and I was desperate for acceptance again. I cajoled and pleaded, and begged to be rewarded by even insincere smiles but for a time, none were forthcoming.

I sit now, alone. With this reflection of my life before me, playing like an old cine film, I recall and digest every scene, each act. It is painful to recall the memories, to see my hourglass almost full at the bottom, and watch the grains of life that are my minutes spraying onto the dune below. The particles, which denote the last of my days, are running out, causing me such heartache, but I know I deserve it.

I can't believe I had a son, I got married, took the vow to love Janice until death we did part and I let it all slip away. It all seems so long ago now. They have all turned on me. I watched as they soared north, free birds much like I once was. I let them go, saw their feathers ruffling in the breeze as they climbed higher, while I dropped south to my now wanted demise. I feel like the end is coming, like I no longer belong here, as if I have no purpose any more.

My eyelids are weary so I let them fall. I long to take the last breath, to end my suffering that I once took pleasure to bestow upon others. That karma exists, I have no doubt. An adage comes to mind. *When God comes calling for his debts there are no I-owe-yous. I suspect I shall burn in Hell.*

I sigh.

He will not let me go. He will not evict me from this prison that is called life.

I will sit and wait, for I have no choice but to do so. I hear God calling to me, but not to unite me within the Heavens. I have sins to repent of. His voice is clear, coming with clarity and an underlying message.

Suffer, child.

I know my time is running out. I have one final act that I must perform before I will bow out gracefully.

And now, I shall tell you all about it.

Chapter Thirty-Nine

George. He had a lot to answer for. But it was my own choice to do what I did, and I don't regret it. Not for one moment.
***

Why had I decided to do this? Why, when I knew how George had sickened me? Was the fact that my own son, a grown man now, a factor in my decision? Was it that I had no one left in my life to love me, or had I thought I could do whatever the hell I wished?

I don't know the answers, but after thinking about George, something inside me wanted to know how it felt to be like him. I wanted to experience something I had so far only witnessed. It was wrong, I *know* that, knew it then, but it fails to matter. I just do it anyway.

So, for two weeks, I watched her from afar. Always at the park next to the school when the educating day was over, she played on the swings, hair flying back in the breeze, eyes closed against the sun, enjoying her freedom.

It wouldn't be long before she would have to leave; her mother arrived to collect her daily at four-thirty.

I don't know why I chose this school. Maybe it was because I had attended it myself at her age, and I knew the surrounding roads and pathways, the places to run, where to hide.

Having seen Edward just the previous evening, it would be a month before he would visit again, and, as he walked away down the path, I knew too that this was possibly the last time I would see my boy.

I thought of him as a child, letting a select few images cross my mind, and when the sting of tears came, when memories from the past threatened to snuff out what I planned to do, I said out loud, "So long, son."

Watching as Edward turned back to wave at me, a lump formed in my throat and then... Stop it! Enough. Let the dark thoughts prevail.

After watching the child for two weeks, I felt I had learned all I needed to know. I had used that time as holiday from work, getting my financial affairs in order, whiling away the hours by writing in my notebook until I could see that child again.

Yes, the words you have read so far have been written while I wait for my time here to end. While writing I've been waiting for a sign to become apparent, to show me which direction to take. I know what I will do now so I'm marching on.

I had an hour before her mother arrived. An hour in which to groom the child some more.

Taking a leaf out of George's book I had approached her last week, laying down the groundwork, throwing the trust over her like a warm, comforting blanket. She took to me, of course she did, a fellow human who loved to swing on swings, who kicked his legs out like she did and threw his head back, laughing.

Just like she did.

The next day I approached her again, but made out I was just walking through the park, waiting for her to ask for my attention. It was easier that way.

"Hey, John!"

She was swinging again, black hair flying in all directions, the wind blowing quite fiercely that day. I glanced up, as if surprised, shielded my eyes as if from the glare of the sun before saying, "Oh, hi!" I waved.

"You coming for a swing?"

I looked at my watch, playing out the charade, and said, "Yes, why not!"

It was three-forty-five p.m.

We swung for a while, laughed and smiled. The ice cream van came by as usual, chime jangling in the air, parking by the railings as it had every day for the past two weeks. She looked over at it longingly.

"You want one?"

She smiled at me, gaps in her teeth, and then dragged her shoes on the tarmac to stop the swing's motion. "Yeah!"

"Come on then. Come and choose what you want. I'll race you!"

And we ran.

The van had a straggle of customers. This was where I should have left it, the fact that this time people had seen me should have been sufficient warning. But no, unstoppable John Brookes pushed on, the urge to complete my cycle too strong to ignore. To make my very own ending was most prevalent in my mind.

Chapter Forty

Hindsight is a wonderful thing, so they say. And indeed it is. She seemed to have no qualms about me whatsoever.

***

"What're you having?" I asked, noting her fair skin, so soft on her plump cheeks.

"A cone with a flake, please!"

She danced from foot to foot, excited, happy, carefree. Her hair pranced with her, pigtails bouncing.

"A cone with a flake it is then! In fact," I turned to smile at her, feeling much like a child myself, "I'm going to have one too!"

She laughed, an infectious giggle that had me joining in, much to the chagrin of the van owner who was leaning palms down on his little counter, looking at me. He looked Greek, his wide arms strong, even for his age, which I guessed at sixty.

"What you want?"

I remember thinking that such an aggressive man really shouldn't run a business visited by children. I also thought that if I had stayed on my previous course, I would have taught the old fool a lesson. But I didn't.

"Two cones with flakes, please."

When he turned his back to pick up the cornets, I poked my tongue out at him, which sent my little companion into fits of giggles.

She really was lovely.

Taking our cornets, I said, "Shall we walk round the outside of the park while we eat them?"

She didn't look at all perturbed, and just said, "Yeah, 'cos by the time we're back, my mam'll be here for me."

"That she will."

After licking her ice cream and pushing her flake down into the cone, she turned to me, white moustache licked off with her small tongue, and said, "I told me mam all about you. She said you sounded nice, and she wished she could swing with me too, but she's too busy working since me dad left."

I didn't want to hear anything about her home life, but the fact she had told her mother gave me a frisson of fear. I didn't want to get caught. I wanted to end this my own way.

"Did she?" I said. "Maybe we could get her on a swing when she comes to pick you up, eh?"

"Nah, can't do that, 'cos she told me not to let you near me again. Said you could be one of them nasty men, so if she sees you at the park again, she'll call the police."

"Oh, right. Well, your mum's quite correct. Tell you what, we'll carry on walking round, and then once we've got back to the park, I'll get off home so you won't get into trouble, yes?"

"Yeah, all right."

I patted her shoulder then to see what her reaction would be and she didn't flinch, just smiled up at me with Jasper eyes.

It was up ahead. The place where I had put *it*, so I switched sides so that I saw it first.

"Oh. Oh, what a shame!"

"What?"

"There. Down there. Will you look at that? How sad!" I went down on my haunches to get a closer look, put my hand over my mouth, shook my head a little.

"Awww, is it all right, John?"

"I don't know. Let's see, shall we?" and I knelt down, checking for signs of life on the kitten that I already knew was dead.

"Is it dead?"

I looked up at her from my kneeling position and nodded. "I'm afraid it is, Clare."

"Should we leave it there?" She looked worried, her eyes were watering, her unfinished cone dropped onto the grass.

"No. That wouldn't be nice. Some other animal may come and eat it later. A badger or fox or some such thing. Best if we bury it, really." I quickly looked at my watch. Half an hour. Picking up the cat, I walked along a little way, Clare following with her head down. She seemed quite upset. "Do you want to wait here while I find somewhere to put it?"

The black and white fur felt warm, but it was only the heat from my own hands giving the illusion of life.

"No, I'll come."

I veered off a little way to a clump of trees where there was a small dip in the ground. "Here, look. We'll lay him in here, shall we?"

Where we stood would probably seem creepy to a child, what with a dead kitten, a relatively strange man and a covering of trees. Her mother's words must have been screaming out to her then. She glanced about nervously.

I realised I had misinterpreted her when she said, "Have we got time? I mean, before me mam comes?"

I looked at my watch.

"Yes, we have around half an hour. Plenty of time. Look, I'll lay him in here then we can collect some small rocks and stones to cover him with. Not much else we can do as we don't have a spade."

"Will he be all right here, though, with just them stones?"

"Oh, I should think so."

I laid the kitten in the hollow and turned to her. "Unless you can get out later on, bring a little hand spade and cover him over."

She thought for a moment. "I can come back later, but we 'ent got a shovel. Not got a garden neither."

"Well that's ok. I have a small spade that should do the trick. What time could you make it back here?" I placed some stones, twigs and leaves on the furry body.

"About seven. I'm allowed out until eight 'cos we only live round the corner. I could get back home in time, couldn't I?"

She helped collect some debris, laying it on top of what I had already done.

"Ok then. I'll meet you back here at seven. We'll bury the poor chap and then you can get off home. How's that sound?"

"Great!" She looked sadly down at the pile of rubble.

"Well then, you've got ten minutes to get yourself back on that swing over there before your mum comes."

"Ok, John." She turned, started running, shouting back, "See you later then?"

"See you later, Clare."

Chapter Forty-One

My course was set. Things were in motion. I couldn't, wouldn't turn back. I wanted to direct my own fate.

***

Before she arrived, I'd uncovered the kitten and dug a similar hole further back in a more secluded place. And then I waited at the original burial spot for her.

Glancing at my watch, I began to get nervous. It was five past seven and she hadn't shown up yet. She had to come, couldn't let me down now that I had psyched myself up, working out how it was to be done, what I would need to carry it all out.

I lit a cigarette—a new habit I had acquired after my father died—to ease my agitation. I blew on the end as I exhaled, and it glowed brighter. As I watched the smoke rise up into the air, I contemplated what I would do if she didn't show.

I needn't have worried for I heard her small footsteps shuffling in the grass. I stood, watching as she emerged through the bushes, head down, walking towards me.

"Hey, Clare," I whispered.

She jumped a little, as if she hadn't really expected me to be there after all.

"I'm a bit late 'cos I had to help me mam with the dishes."

How old was this child? No more than eight I would guess, helping her mother do the dishes. I wondered if she had called out to

167

Clare to be careful when she was out. Whether she hugged and kissed her when she left or if she was so relieved to get some peace and quiet that she slumped down on her chair with a vodka and tonic and a cigarette, relishing in the stillness around her, the very air of home soothing away the day's unrest.

"That's all right, Clare, don't you worry. Now then, let's get this kitten buried so that you can get home, eh?"

She looked down at the ground then, confusion flitting across her small features, eyes narrowing as she tried to work out what was different. When realisation dawned, her eyes sprang wide.

"Where's he gone?" She looked up at me questioningly.

"Well, I've had to move him, you see. While we were gone, an animal seemed to have been sniffing around as some of the stones were moved. I thought it would be best to bury him properly. What do you think?"

She nodded, glancing round the small clearing, shoulders hunched with the small thrill of fear that comes when a nighttime sound startles you. "What was that?" she asked.

"Probably that nasty little animal coming back," I replied in a soothing tone. "Come on, the sooner we bury this kitty, the better. This way, just over here."

She followed quickly, wanting to be near me in case the animal made an appearance, I suppose. Funny how to her mind the unseen noisemaker held more of a threat than me. Oh, the simplicity of an immature mind.

I led her to a tree where the boughs grew low, low enough for me to touch when I tied the rope there. I wound it round the sturdy branch and concealed it. My bag leant against the vast trunk, the zip open for easy access.

"Here, look. I started with the shovel before you came. Made quite a deep hole for the kitten, see?"

The hole was indeed deep, around three feet, the opening big enough to fit in a kitten and the other things I had in mind. Ensconced as we were within this little wooded area, it really had worked out rather well, so any fear I had previously felt was now gone. Feeling that it was meant to be, I watched as Clare peered down into the hole.

"Nothing will get him in there, will it?" she asked, smiling. "They'd have to dig for a long time to reach him, wouldn't they?"

"They would, so don't you worry. Once we've covered him up and stamped down the earth, he'll be safe."

I moved closer to the tree, reached out and got my shovel, walking behind her. "Shall we put him in the hole then?"

"Ok." Bravely she picked up the kitten and kneeled down beside the hole. "I can't reach to put him in, so I'll have to drop him."

"I'm sure that will be fine." I glanced at my watch. She had forty-three minutes left before she had to be home. I started to get a little impatient.

I heard the body hit the bottom of the grave and dug my shovel into the mound of earth next to it, scattering some mud over the furry corpse. Clare helped by taking handfuls of sod and throwing it into the hole, concentration evident on her face. She wanted to do this right.

While she was busy, I rested my shovel back against the trunk, and then made my way behind her as she threw in one more handful.

"You gonna help me, John?"

I don't want to describe what I did next as thinking about it now makes me ashamed of myself. Years ago, I killed a baby but I tell myself I was young, that I didn't really know what I was doing. That the reasons for doing what I did to that baby seemed right at the time, and it wasn't until we had Edward that I realised how vulnerable small children are and that I had done a terrible thing to my brother.

With Clare, well, I was an adult, and so intent was I to commit that last crime that I didn't *think* properly about what I was doing. Oh, I had planned what I wanted to do to Clare, but it didn't seem real somehow. It was like it was something being done by someone else and I was just watching.

Even when I committed my crime, I went through the motions as if it was an every day thing and not the terrible act that it was. I remember wishing that life had been different for me, that someone had done to me what I had done to Clare and then all those people I had snuffed out would still be alive, carrying on with their dreams and their longings. We all have them, don't we?

169

I don't know where I went wrong. When the rage and the urges overtook me I didn't listen to reason. The beast in me ignored the tiny voice that sometimes whispered in my ear that I had done a very bad thing. I felt unstoppable at those times and nothing anyone could have said would have made me change my mind.

Perhaps it is my age that made me regret Clare. Perhaps it was the fact that I had taken away the life of someone's child, and the mother would feel enormous grief when her daughter was discovered.

It's times like this that I want to end it all. I want to stop my own life as well, but I know I don't have the courage for that. I must be punished, I know this. I would kill myself but I'm a coward. Ironic that I'm afraid to commit suicide yet can kill someone else with ease.

I remember saying to her, "You were a good girl, Clare. Now everything will be all right. I just have to do this one thing and everything will be fine. I need to do this. Have to."

Why I felt the need to say this, I don't know. Perhaps I was trying to justify what I was about to do.

She looked up at me, dark brown Jasper eyes pleading for my mercy. Her tear-streaked face will stay with me forever. Then something took over me again, that *thing* inside me grew and once again... I. Did. Not. Care.

Chapter Forty-Two

The noose swung slightly in the breeze. I found it ironic that she liked to swing and would do so with her dying breath.

***

Taking the large bottle of water from my bag, I began cleaning up. Dousing the shovel with the water, I threw it into the hole with the kitten, hearing the thud. Collecting the ball of string, I wet that too, and threw that down into the grave. I kicked the soil back into the hole, burying that wretched cat for good.

Smoothing the ground, I felt sure I had erased all my footprints, all evidence that I was ever there. Forensics slipped through my mind, but I swept those thoughts away. It didn't matter anymore.

It was done.

I turned and made my way out of the clearing, walking in full view across the park. Though dark, I was sure someone must have seen me, but it was only a fleeting thought. I had been lucky thus far, so why not now too?

Opening the small gate farthest from Clare's eternal swing, I emerged onto the path, scuffing my shoes as I walked to remove the mud. I might have appeared a normal man, backpack bouncing, lit cigarette hanging from my lips, or I could have seemed strange.

A little "off".

I made my way back to the cabin, getting out my notebook so that I could add the last entries. Everything would be there for them. I didn't want to have to explain it all, reliving it when writing has made me see myself in a different light. I'm struggling now, struggling to comprehend it all.

I knew when I began writing this that I wouldn't feel remorse. Everything previous to Clare had seemed right.

Now I feel differently. There was something about that last act that brought it all home. How can I adore my son the way I do yet take that little girl's life? There *is* something wrong with me; I know that now. It's like Clare broke that *thing* in my brain that wasn't working properly and I can finally *see* the truth in all its hideousness. I wish that I had been shown this before...

I will never reveal Clare's last moments for I cannot bear to go through them again myself. I am and have been a monster. I am not fit to walk round a free man. Taking my own life is too frightening and isn't what I deserve.

Hell was on my mind a lot during the walk back from the park. I don't want to go there or see my mother again. Not just yet. So I think living a hell on Earth is better.

I will leave this notebook out on the table for them to find, and if I'm lucky, they will let me have another one so that I can continue with my story. But for now, it is goodbye.

Epilogue

I sit here on a cheap, grey plastic chair. The walls are bare except for the many finger marks and grubby patches from equally grubby people. A table, chipped and scarred, bearing witness to many humiliations, sits in the centre of the room. A tape recorder, ears of the righteous, spools turning, immortalises my voice. I belong here.

"John. Tell us. From the beginning," an investigator says.

"The beginning?" I bark out a nervous laugh. "*Right* from the start? Dear fellow that would take far too long!"

They try to make me uneasy with their unwavering stares. The beginnings of tremendous guilt burrows into my soul, and for the first time, I truly realise that I *have* a soul. If I didn't, I wouldn't feel this horrible sensation spearing me through the chest. I wonder if I will be able to cope with the reverse of what I have so far experienced. Before, I had no remorse my entire life. Now, it seems I have plenty.

I take a packet from the table, languidly select a cigarette, light it, and draw smoke deep into my lungs, enjoying the head rush. It steadies me.

"We've got as long as it takes."

Retrieving the images from my mind is like flicking through a much handled photo album. I know who belongs on which page. I can close my eyes, read the edges like Braille, and know which of my actions will be smiling out at me in the place I've selected. Except I don't want to view them anymore. Do not want to see.

Yet I go back in my mind once more, to the operations on the birds, the torture of Twinkle the cat, and the gutting of the fish on the

173

banks with my father. I see the drowning of my half-brother and death of my mother. Cine film whizzes past my line of vision, I can see it all as if it were yesterday, and sometimes, it really feels as if it is.

They want to know about the child, her name. I don't want to talk about her for if I do the pain will come but I still tell them.

"Clare."

"Was she the only child you killed, John?"

"No."

I smile.

"Why are you smiling, John?"

I look at them with disdain. They really don't understand. They really have no idea what has been going through my mind all my life and what is going through it now. I don't know why I smiled, nerves maybe? It is alien to me to feel such fear.

"What happened when Clare came to meet you at the park, John?"

"I don't want to talk about it."

"Come on now, John. You walked in here, gave yourself up, man! You can't expect not to tell us what we need to know!"

"I killed her, all right? I killed her."

The images are as sharp as the day I'd stored them. Kodak fresh. And they hurt. I'm so surprised about that. I left the cabin earlier, and left everything as I wanted it found and walked here, to the police station. I took a deep breath before I pushed open the double glass doors, thought about Father, Janice and Edward, how I had let them all down, the people who had loved me. I decided it was right, what I was about to do.

I walked up to the desk and the police officer didn't look up when he said, "Can I help you?" He was busy filling out a form.

"My name is John Brookes, and I have come to tell you that I have killed people."

The policeman looked up then. His face was startled, and I'm certain he was unsure what to do next.

"Have you, sir?" He lifted the hatch on the desk and said, "Would you like to come with me. I'll get someone you can talk to."

I felt like crying, my heart hammered, my mouth went dry, and bile rose. The urge came upon me to admit what I had done so I said,

"There is a little girl swinging by a noose from a tree in the park nearby. Her name is Clare."

He didn't answer me, just led me to this room as he spoke into his radio that was attached to his uniform jacket.

And then these two men came in and started asking me questions, and I wanted to cry, I really did. For all the things I had done, for the things done to me, for the confusion as a child, oh, for every damn thing.

One of the officers continues now, bringing me out of my thoughts, "Moving backwards. What about at the park, John, what happened there last week?"

I sigh. They won't understand. They won't believe me either if I express remorse, not after they find my notebook and see what else I have done. And I don't blame them.

"What do *you* think? You're the detectives! You tell *me*!" I say this wearily. I'm tired, so tired.

"Well, John. I think you took an innocent child, Clare Moore to be more specific, and killed her. We *know* that. What we *don't* know, is why. Or how many other kids you may have got your hands on."

"No other children, none of any importance anyway. Just her. You need to go to my home. Get my notebook. Everything is in there."

I don't want to talk about it because if I do, if I start to say it, I know I will cry. I'll cry like I should have done when I was a child and it'll all come out and I don't want it to. I just want to suffer in silence.

"Let's go back then, John. Back to the very beginning, all right? Back to the first person you killed because you mentioned that, didn't you, when we first came in, that you wanted to talk about the first one."

"Get the notebook. Read the notebook."

"John, we need *you* to tell us what happened. For the tape."

I don't respond, just look at the tabletop and see the images flicking, flicking through my mind, tormenting me. I see the rope and close my eyes to make it go away but it is there again behind closed eyelids.

"We need you to tell us, for the tape. All the details."

175

I sigh again. "If it isn't too much trouble, I would like a break. A cup of tea. Two sugars."

"That's fine, John."

I take another cigarette and one of the policemen says, "Come on, John. Tell us what happened. You'll have to eventually, you know."

I stay silent, watch my own movie playing in the space before me, something they can't see unless I choose to tell them. And it is horrific. Now it seems terrible, horrendous. What the hell have I been *doing* all these years? Where has this sorrow for what I have done sprung from?

"John!" barks the other officer, who has so far stayed silent. They seem to be getting impatient with me.

My eyes have glazed over. I shake my head to clear my mind, open my mouth to tell them...

She pissed herself, kicked at me. So I strung her up in that tree.

"May I have that break now? Please can I have some tea, have the tape turned off?"

They bring the tea. I am quite surprised it is hot. The steam rises in curls from the polystyrene cup.

"Now then, John. We would like to know about the first time you ever hurt someone. We know Clare wasn't your first. Come on now, John. Get it all out, over and done with."

The more silent of the officers gets up from his chair. He is pacing, pacing. I look at his clenched fists.

"Where are they all, John? Tell us. *Who* are they?"

I hold up my hand, my index finger pointing skyward, indicating that they wait, give me a little time. I am finding it hard to swallow and spittle pools in my mouth.

I give in, whisper, "In a better place."

The silent officer lurches forward, slams his clenched fist upon the desk. I can't believe he has grabbed my shirt in his hand, and that his fist, the fist that just struck the table, is pulled back, ready to strike me!

A part of the old indignant me returns, "If you hit me, you will be in much trouble, you know that, don't you?"

176

He releases his grip, drops his fist. He stands back, straightening his tie, and fiddles with the knot. His face is rather on the red side. Then he lunges again.

"Mark! No, stop!" The talkative one has spoken. Silent Mark steps back once again.

Blue. Her face was puffed and blue.

"Interview suspended, five fifteen p.m."

Detective Talkalot nods at Silent Mark, and I know I am done. I have achieved what I set out to do, have taken my own path, struggled against my inner demons and given myself up, gone my *own* way. I have gone one step further, pushed the boundaries and got myself caught up now in remorse and conscience. I can't keep killing people. I have acted out my life.

My pervalism.

BIO

M. E Ellis is married with five children and resides in the U.K. She has written several novels and over three hundred short stories. Although she writes in several genres, her books are predominantly horror based.

Turn the page for an excerpt from M.E Ellis'
psychological thriller novel:

Quits

Available as an ebook at Wild Child Publishing
http://www.wildchildpublishing.com/

Chapter One

Alarm. Toilet. Dress.

Breakfast. Coffee. Door.

Car. Drive. Arrive.

Every damn day.

I could say I enjoy the lighter side of life—the drinks after work, exchanging banter with the co-workers, the in-jokes—but I don't. It's all well and good when that's all that floats your boat. I bumble along and I try to stay relaxed. But it isn't enough. My mind is screaming for something, anything but the monotony of every day.

I'm a bloke, right? The world should go back to basics, strip life back to the way it used to be. I should be the provider, able to fend for myself and make my own way through this world. I hear women talking sometimes. It sounds like they act like men, with their beer swilling antics. Their loud maws protesting their sameness when all along they *are* different.

I don't think women face their fears or think rationally when something scares them. No, I think they scream, rant and rave and act like the girls they are and *still* they always want to be both a man *and* a woman—when it suits them, and isn't that always the way? When it suits, when they're ready, or when they feel comfortable with it.

I hear stories about how they cock-suck some fellow one minute and fob him off the next. A woman will tease a guy's prick like there's no tomorrow, then withdraw when it looks like she's got the bloke under her thumb.

I'm going to perform an experiment and see how far it goes before I prove my point. I'll bet it doesn't take long either. I'll bet she'll be screaming and squirming inside of a minute. Besides, I've got nothing better to do.

I know who the subject will be too. I've seen her around from time to time. It was a choice between two birds who hang out together. They meet one another each night outside the coffee shop, strutting up and down the sidewalk like hardened pros. Once, they were even approached by some old duffer in a suit who propositioned them, saying cash was no object.

The gals giggled when he walked off and he realised his folly. I bet they twittered to each other about looking old enough to *be* prossers. Eighteen or so years of age, looking twenty-five. Make-up does that to a female—that and the right attire. Of course, the way they're brought up these days doesn't help, maturing too fast. Society drags them along by the reins like some racehorse at the Grand National. The girls are the jockeys, hanging on for dear life, gripping the horse's flanks at the hurdles, hurdles that grow in height as the females age, vast mountains to climb before real womanhood appears.

So I've chosen the one who looks more pliable, yet at the same time, she has a tough look to her. She acts like she knows where she's at, where she's going, who she wants to be. Ain't anyone going to stop *her*.

Except me.

Printed in the United Kingdom
by Lightning Source UK Ltd.
135776UK00002B/187/A